Las Vegas Luck

LOVE IN THE BIG APPLE
BOOK 1.5

NICOLE SANCHEZ

To request permissions, contact the author at author.nicolesanchez@gmail.com

First paperback edition September 2022

Copyright Registration Number TX 9-204-460

Edited by Amanda Iles

Cover Art by Angela Haddon Designs

Vector Image by Vecteezy.com

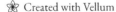 Created with Vellum

For anyone all those who have had a memorable bachelorette or bachelor party, this one is for you

One

AINSLEY

"YOU'VE BEEN A VERY naughty girl. Clearly, detention wasn't enough for you to learn your lesson. It's time for a different sort of punishment."

My eyes roll so far back into my head, I think they might get stuck like that. To keep up the ruse that I'm enjoying this, I throw in what I hope is a convincing moan as Martin pumps into me. He slaps my ass, grunting with each movement. My mind is trying to focus on the moment, trying to pull pleasure from him, but instead I remember that I forgot to send Eloise a revised agreement for the couple treating their houseboat in Amsterdam like a timeshare.

Focus, Ainsley, focus.

"Harder," I plead, but too late. I know that my voice lacks the appropriate emotion.

Whoops.

Martin stops, and I'm a little grateful for it. Maybe I can call it a night. Hooking up with him had seemed like a good idea, but when I started running through my to-do list for tomorrow I realized that I didn't actually want to do this.

When I swiped on Martin's profile, I didn't expect the

1

phrase "Always available to learn a lesson" to be indicative of his sexual proclivities. He's cute in that helpless puppy sort of way, with thick glasses that usually have me soaking my panties, but this is the second date where he hasn't stopped talking about himself. If we were on a game show and he was asked to give five facts about me that didn't have to do with my name or my appearance, we would lose. Meanwhile, I know that his first pet's name was Tallulah, his third grade teacher was Mrs. Elroy and the street he grew up on was Astor Drive. I'm ready to hack his life.

"Ainsley?" He doesn't want to stop, and for a moment I weigh if it's worth it to just keep going.

No. No, it's not worth it. My brain keeps drifting to thoughts of my day tomorrow and my third meeting with a couple that keeps using me as a marriage counselor instead of a divorce mediator. Not that I can object when they keep signing checks.

I step forward before standing up straight, so he's forced to pull out. It's not that I don't like Martin, it's just that I don't see this going anywhere past a handful of dates and mediocre sex. I'm on the Sleepless Nights app for some fun hookups, but I invariably ask myself if I see these trysts as more than just a hookup.

Squatting with my knees closed, I pull up my panties, straightening them out. A quick once-over of my clothes confirms that while I *was* screwing in the bathroom, it doesn't *look* like I've been screwing in a bathroom. My pencil skirt has the appropriate wrinkles from being worn all day. Quickly, I re-button the two undone buttons on my blouse before I face Martin.

"I'm sorry, I'm not sure that this is working," I confess. Nothing about Martin makes my heart twist in anticipation of something more, like waking up nestled in his arms on a Saturday morning. I don't blame him for the confused look on his face. When we started chatting, I wasn't looking for this to be anything more than a casual occasional hookup, but even that has been unfulfilling.

"Not working?" He sounds genuinely confused but makes no move to tuck his increasingly deflated dick in his pants.

There is a chuckle that wants to work its way out when I notice that his smile and hardness are directly correlated. The more his smile falls, the softer his dick. It's such an inappropriate response that I cough into my fist to hide my laugh.

I grab my purse from where it rests on the counter. "Yeah, if you're already pulling out the teacher-student roleplay on the second date, then you have a lot kinkier shit in your closet. And while I do not yuck anyone's yum, this isn't my flavor. You seem like a nice guy, but—"

"But I'm not your type? It's not me, it's you?" Martin is hastily tucking his shirt back into his pants, along with his cock. "Yeah, you're a fucking tease, so I believe that."

"Wow, not what I was going to say, but thanks for mansplaining your rejection to me. It is definitely you."

I don't bother letting him get dressed before I throw open the bathroom door. It swings shut behind me with a slam as I strut out into the wine bar and leave him with the open bar tab.

Vivian is on the phone when I walk into my apartment. Her dark brown eyes meet mine with an eye roll as she gestures to her phone. On the table in front of her is her planner, the one I've come to dread seeing. The wedding planner, in its white and gold finery, is stuffed with inspirational magazine cutouts, business cards and color swatches. The organization skills this woman has bring a whole new meaning to the phrase "planner whore." I think she has three, one for her personal needs, one for work, and this one for the wedding.

"Yeah, no, I totally understand." She sounds dejected as she leans back, wrapping the end of her ponytail around her fist, angrily tugging on it. "Yeah, hmmm, okay. I get it. Elia will understand. I'll give you the address for sending a card. Thanks. It was good to catch up. Yeah, mmmm, okay, bye!" Her voice is full of fake cheer.

Vivian makes sure the call has ended before she screams at her phone. She drops it on the table with a loud thunk, her cheeks pink with frustration. At some point, she's going to drop her phone with enough force to break the glass top table. I wince before striding into the kitchen and grabbing a bottle of wine and two glasses.

"What asinine wedding task is making you batty tonight?"

For weeks, Vivian has bent herself over backwards trying to get everything ready for her best friend's wedding. I want to offer to help, but it gets awkward when her best friend, Elia, is marrying my ex-fiancé, Charlie. Truly, I think I might be the one overcomplicating things, but I have my reasons.

It doesn't help that Elia and I got off on a bad foot when she and Charlie first started dating. Our mutual friend Jack convinced me that Charlie wanted to get back together, so I made a fool of myself trying to win him back. I didn't even want Charlie anymore. We've mended bridges, but we're hardly slumber party besties.

Shit hit the fan on Valentine's day earlier this year when it came out just how far Jack was willing to manipulate everyone, including his fiancé, Vivian, to keep them apart. It was pretty amazing to see Jack get what he deserved when Vivian broke up with him.

While Elia has said she's okay with me, I'm still her fiancé's ex. It gets a little awkward when you've both boned the same guy.

Vivian sighs. "It's not asinine. I volunteered to help. If it was up to Elia, she wouldn't do anything, no shower, no bachelorette, no rehearsal. She and Charlie would go to the courthouse and call it a day."

"If that's what she wants, then why not do that?" I pour us each a large glass, never mind that I already had a bottle of my own at the wine bar with Martin.

"Because it's not really what she wants. She doesn't want to take advantage of Charlie's money for something extravagant and she doesn't feel close to enough people that she would want to have a big party."

I wince, remembering that Elia is still dealing with memory problems after the accident that connected her and Charlie. Memories have been coming back, but she's admitted to Vivian that, at this point, she likely won't get many more. What she has gotten are slivers, little pieces of her history. The rest of her memory is otherwise lost.

"So, what's the problem?"

Vivian takes a long pull from her wine glass. "Elia and I have over fifty sorority sisters, and I can't get a single one to agree to come. It doesn't help that this is all, like, super last minute."

"This is hardly last minute; it's August. Aren't they getting married in December? You have four months. The bachelorette also doesn't have to be some big weekend in Macau or Paris or something. You can always go to Napa or Atlantic City or Vegas."

The glare Vivian gives me tells me that this was the wrong thing to say. I knew Vivian in passing before her breakup with Jack left her without somewhere to stay. I had more than enough space in my place to harbor a fellow victim of her ex. That was seven months ago. I'm not eager to kick her out. I don't want to. As much as living with someone else again has been an adjustment, it's been nice having someone to come home to and talk about my day with.

I crave that connection and I want it again, just not with Vivian. I want someone to hold me while they stroke my hair and tell me about their day.

"It's just not enough time to put together a quality bachelorette and bridal shower and help with the actual wedding. I have, like, no time to plan this and have my own life."

"So I ask again, why are you taking all this on? I know Elia and I haven't spent a ton of time together, but from what I've seen, she's a good friend and would understand you not stretching yourself thin over this."

Vivian drains her glass, reaching to fill it again. Having her as my roommate has seriously blown up my wine budget, not just because there is someone else drinking, but because drinking with a friend is a lot more responsible than finishing a bottle by myself like I did before she moved in.

"I need to do this to make it up to her. I *want* to do this."

I choke back my sigh by draining my glass. "What do I know about weddings? I never made it down the aisle."

"Oh, and I do? I've only failed to tie the knot *twice*." She finishes her second glass just as quickly, and I know I've hit a nerve.

Vivian reaches for the wine to fill her now empty glass again, but I grab it instead. "That first one doesn't count. What was his name? Cormac? Chris? Carmine?"

I'm hoping I can get her to laugh or smile or something that isn't choking down alcohol. I would call her out on it, point out how drowning your worries in booze isn't the answer, but I'm afraid of her holding a mirror up to me, reminding me of my own flaws.

The truth is, I wish I was married, but I need to get myself in order before I can even think about that. The future I had envisioned for myself was full of kids with a partner who was there through it all. I miss having that one person in my life who was there for everything. I'm not getting any younger, and if I want to have kids on my own, I really need to consider what I have to do to get there. For now, I'll keep using Sleepless Nights. And if I meet someone worth more than just a few quick fucks, great! If not, I'll figure it out. I've always prided myself on being able to adapt.

"Connor. We were engaged longer than Jack and I were."

"And he was shitty." I grab her hand and squeeze it.

"Maybe I'm just shitty at picking men." Vivian looks into her wine glass like it holds all the answers.

"Pfft. I find that hard to believe. You're excellent at picking friends."

"It doesn't change that I can't get anyone to come to the bachelorette. I can't even get a noncommittal, 'Send me the details.' They're all flat-out rejections."

"I'm sure I can make some calls and see if I know anyone that's available for a good time. Talk to Charlie and Taryn. I'm sure if it comes down to money, Charlie will foot the bill if it means having more people. Though it doesn't sound like Elia wants more people."

"But she does! When we were in college she was the first one at the bar or on a table while we were dancing. She loves to party, and I think she'll be a little sad if it's just Taryn and me. When we first moved to the city, we were always there for last call at the bar near our apartment."

"I'm sure you'll figure it out. There must be at least one or two other people you know who love to party."

Vivian lifts her head from the table and regards me, canting her head to the side, and I don't think I like the look on her face.

Two

ELIA

CHARLIE HAS me pinned to the kitchen counter, his lips trailing along my neck to nip at my ear. His hands are braced on either side of me, leaving me with no other option than to accept these kisses. Months ago, this would have left me feeling trapped, with Charlie backing off immediately until I felt comfortable again. It's taken a lot of therapy to help me get back to a place where I can feel love in these moments instead of terror.

"Stop. Vivian is going to be here in, like, ten minutes," I object with a giggle, a perfunctory protest at best. The truth is, I don't want to stop. I want to feel him touching me constantly, his body pressed to mine.

My fiancé's hands drop down to my thighs, so he can lift me. Instinctively, my legs wrap around his waist.

"Just means I have to act fast." His mouth captures mine as he presses his erection against my core. I'll never get over how perfect we fit together.

My objections are half-hearted as I lean into him, wrapping my arms around his shoulders. I catch a glimpse of my engagement ring as I hold him to me. The three carat solitaire is more than I ever expected. I tried to tell him I didn't need anything this elaborate, but there was no convincing him otherwise. He honestly could have gotten me something from a department store and I would have been happy knowing that he was going to be my husband. We've been working on trying to temper his extravagances with my more humble upbringing. The world I came from is so different from his. I actually spit my coffee out on him when he told me that not only does he have a car in Manhattan, but that it's an entirely ostentatious cherry red Porsche Spyder that he bought right after graduating college that he drives once a year. When I graduated, I was happy to buy an old Nissan with over 150,000 miles on it.

Charlie's hips press against me, and I want more, so I roll my hips in equal measure. His whole body is so powerful, and he's demonstrated just how strong he is day in and out. I thought we were insatiable in Bora Bora, but ever since we got engaged, we've barely kept our clothes on.

The knock on our door puts an end to our playing.

"That's Vivian," I whisper against his swollen lips.

Charlie presses his forehead against mine. "Maybe if we stay quiet, she'll go away and I can show you what it takes to be Mr. Eligible."

I snort at his mention of her reason for coming. Every Monday night, we get together to watch women compete for their happily ever after on a reality show. Is it real? Maybe not. Do we care? Not a chance.

"Would you horn dogs let me in?" Vivian calls through the door. There is another loud thunk, which I imagine is her head as she leans against it. This isn't the first time we've been caught with our pants down when she got here and I doubt it will be the last.

I giggle while Charlie groans into my neck. One last little nip before he releases me.

"I'm going to go take care of this." He gestures between us at the erection straining against his sweats. I grip him and give him a hard stroke over his pants. Charlie doesn't touch me, but his head drops back in frustration. The sound he makes almost has me forgetting about my friend, but she's been doing so much for me that I can't leave her hanging.

"I'll be thinking of you," I promise, twisting out of his arms. My husband-to-be slips into our bedroom while I go to greet my best friend.

"So will I," he mutters under his breath, closing our bedroom door with bang. My cheeks flush, wishing I was the one giving him pleasure.

Vivian grins when I open the door.

"Charlie just jumped in the shower," I tell her by way of greeting. I want to reach up and touch my lips, feel if she can see the bruises I imagine are there.

"I totally interrupted you fucking, didn't I?" Vivian asks before throwing her arms around me.

"Almost, but that's fine. It's not like we're starved for sex."

Vivian lets out a wistful sigh. "Tell me more about this sex you're having. Ainsley regals me with tales of her one-night stands. It's the closest I'm getting to action these days."

Her recent heartbreak with Jack makes me more aware of how much effort she's been putting into planning all of my various wedding activities. I appreciate everything that she has been doing, but a part of me wonders if she's throwing herself so entirely into it because she should have been planning her own nuptials. When she started asking feeler questions about what I wanted for my shower and bachelorette, I froze a little because all I've thought about is seeing Charlie at the end of the aisle.

"What about your trusty vibrator?"

"That pleasure can only go so far."

"You could always date again?" I suggest. It's not the first time I've proposed it, but her reaction is always the same.

Vivian's mouth purses like she's tasted something sour. "No, no men for me. I jumped from Connor to Jack, and I think that's a sign that I should just go without men for a while. Sex is nice, but so is having a glass of wine for myself without having to fold someone else's boxers."

"Play your cards right, and I'll sign you up for Mr. Eligible."

Vivian throws her purse on the island, shaking her head. "No, thank you, ma'am. I want no part of having my relationship on TV."

"You never know who you're going to fall in love with," I point out. "Could be Mr. Perfect is already someone you know." I wiggle my eyebrows suggestively.

"I'll eat my hat if it's this new attorney I'm dealing with. There's a better chance of it being Mr. Eligible, and you know I refuse to even go on the show."

Behind me, I hear the shower turn off and smirk to myself, knowing that Charlie had me on his mind while he had himself in hand.

Vivian sits on the couch while I pull a fresh bottle of wine out of the wine fridge. We've done this often enough that we have a routine down pat. Moments like this make me glad that Vivian and I reconnected. There is a lot of water under the bridge from when we lost touch in the last five years, and we haven't really talked about that. What it was like for me to let Vivian, a woman I considered my sister, basically walk out of my life. There is plenty of blame to go around when it comes to what happened and none of it falls on us.

I set out a charcuterie board and make popcorn. Monday nights are not for eating a real dinner. They're for eating meats and cheese and popcorn while drinking a bottle of wine. The first time Vivian and I did this, Charlie was shocked by the lack of nutrients we were eating, and since then he has tried to sneak things like fruit and vegetables onto the board while muttering something about scurvy.

Charlie emerges with his blond hair still damp. His alma mater's shirt clings to his wet chest and his sweatpants hang low on his hips. I nearly drop the wine bottle in my hands as I look at him.

There is a thin gap between his shirt and his sweats showcasing his Adonis belt and the finely-toned muscles and I actually stop breathing as I watch him run a towel through his hair. There is a special sort of glee in knowing that all of that is all mine.

He catches my reaction and smiles, winking at me like the devil he is before turning to Vivian. "Hey, Viv."

"Charlie Brown," she teases.

Charlie presses a kiss to my temple, grabbing the charcuterie board and wine glasses to help me. "What's this I hear about you going on a date with some attorney?"

My heart melts with how he leans into conversations with my friend. It's hard to remember that during my missing five years, they knew each other. Charlie had withheld that he knew Vivian to avoid pressuring me unnecessarily, and at that time I was mad that it felt like one more thing he held back from me. In the end, I was glad that he let me get back to Vivian on my own terms. With how much everyone was poking and prodding at our relationship, I needed someone in my corner who felt like they were mine.

"Yeah, he's some dickhead. The partners took on a real estate deal for a big client and stuck me with it because I did Charlie's condo way back when. Only now, I'm doing an entire building, with leases and a construction loan. The attorney on the other side is dragging it out, and it sounds like even after we finish the sale, there is some sort of deal linking the seller and buyer. My bosses have basically sold me to this guy for the foreseeable future."

"What's his name?"

"Knox Benedict. He even sounds like a prick." The disgust in Vivian's voice makes me laugh.

"If you're in need of a good fuck, sounds like a hate bang might be perfect," I point out with a shrug.

Charlie snorts into his wine glass, reserving any comment when it comes to telling Vivian how to live her life. He always pretends like he's not invested in the show, but he joins in our commercial break commentary. It's not because he thinks he's above a show like Mr. Eligible, but because he wants to give me and Vivian space to reconnect. We really have come together again so much, but sometimes I think she's still a little worried I'm going to flake on her after how everything with Bryan went down the first time. I wouldn't let it happen again, even if I can't remember the details of how we grew apart, and Charlie won't allow history to repeat either.

We settle into our usual seats to watch the opening, picking up from the end of the last episode where the lead is breaking up a physical fight between women over the glass slipper he gives to the girls he wants to stay. The slipper in question shatters, leading to both women looking on tearily as they're dismissed.

Bonsai and Mochi, the kittens that Charlie got as Christmas presents, always come to snug with Vivian when she's here, and tonight is no exception. Mochi takes up her post on the pillow behind Vivian's head while Bonsai plops right in her lap.

We're halfway through the show when Vivian turns to me during a commercial break. I know the face she's making. It usually comes before she throws a crazy idea at me. Like making jello shots with jungle juice or trying bangs again.

"How do you feel about inviting Ainsley to brunch with us this weekend?" She's trying to keep her tone casual as she grabs the bottle of wine. Her entire focus is on refilling all of our glasses, giving Charlie and me a chance to carry on a silent conversation.

Our eyes meet over her head. We have a volley, silently asking if the other is okay with this without as many words. I like Ainsley, I really do. She's smart and funny and able to pick up on things most people miss unless she's being led astray. It's part of what makes her a great divorce mediator, if what I've heard has any truth to it.

Charlie gives a small lift to his shoulder, leaving it up to me. She was a good friend to Charlie after we broke up briefly and even took Vivian in when she was left suddenly homeless after her engagement with Jack ended. So many abandoned fiancés in our lives, I sometimes find it hard to keep track.

Vivian sits back and faces me, handing over my now full wine glass. I chew on my lip, wondering how to proceed.

"So, I've talked a little with my therapist about Ainsley and everything that happened. She's obviously a big part of what went down this winter and even more, she's a big part of your life now." I focus on Charlie, trying to call to mind the conversations we've had. "She's pointed out that while Ainsley's actions were her own, it's unfair to judge her based on the things she did while being manipulated, the same way it would be unfair for you to judge me for how I was after everything that happened with Bryan. She also pointed out that Ainsley's actions after Valentine's day are a better judge of who she is as a person.

"I've wanted to reach out to her, but honestly felt awkward about it."

Charlie reaches out and pauses the TV so I can keep going uninterrupted. I want to kiss him for it.

Vivian is patient, waiting for me to decide. The truth is, when Ainsley and I have crossed paths, we've both kept it civil and perfunctory, not wanting to impose our presence on the other for too long. That's how it is on my end, and I'm assuming she's thought the same. It's always felt awkward being the woman that Charlie is settling down with, the woman he left his job for when he wouldn't do the same for her.

When I first started going to therapy, it was something that I kept to myself. It felt like I was admitting some sort of personal failure by telling people I started to see a therapist. But there is nothing wrong with it, and so many people can benefit from having somewhere safe to talk through their problems. I encouraged Charlie to go as well, as he tries to repair the relationship with his mother and brother. When he admitted to me that he went for the first time, I hugged him fiercely as I swelled with pride.

Charlie was the one who convinced me that it was okay to let people in on that if I wanted to. He was right. It wasn't a personal failure to go to therapy; lord knows I needed it. The number of things I had to and still have to work through when it comes to what happened with Bryan and my accident means I'll be keeping my therapist in business all on my own.

"So, yeah, I would be totally okay with it." I release the pent-up breath I was holding. "Sorry, that was a very roundabout way of saying that."

Vivian smiles and squeezes my knee, "Good, because I think you could both use a new friend."

I'm early for brunch that weekend. I can't pinpoint why I'm so anxious. Actually, that's not entirely true; I can pinpoint it. I know that it's because part of me wants to make a good impression. It's the peacekeeper in me that wants to make nice with my best friend's roommate. Still, it feels like there is a vice on my chest, slowly suffocating me.

I'm firing off texts to Charlie, who has done nothing but encourage me to do what I feel is right. He's offered to send a car if I change my mind, but I'm not going to. It's more than just knowing that Ainsley was just as wronged. It's knowing that if we hadn't been pitted against each other, we could have been friends. It's knowing that she's been a good friend to the people most important to me and if they love her or loved her at some point, then there is something worthy about her.

"Els!" Taryn shouts, coming up behind me. She hugs me tightly, squeezing until I cry for mercy. I spin around to face my red-haired friend, who I feel like I never see. Our friendship is similarly new, but we keep it going by sharing funny videos and memes.

Since she started her internship at the beginning of summer, we've hardly seen her. I know that she's been working ridiculous hours. Charlie told me that this is just the industry she chose — investment banking. Taryn wanted to do it on her own, so she refused to reach out to Charlie for help getting an internship. It was for the best since Charlie wound up leaving his job at his father's firm when we found out that his father was working with Jack to get me out of Charlie's life for good.

"Hey, pretty lady," I say, turning in her arms.

"I hear we have a special guest joining us?" she asks, looping her arm with mine.

Taryn used to work at Claudia Jean's, our go-to brunch spot, and has said she will probably go back in the fall. This is her first day off from her internship in six weeks, which is thankfully ending soon. I don't blame her for not being able to juggle a second job. I'm pretty sure she would need a time machine just to get sleep.

"Yes, Vivian asked if Ainsley could come. I'm surprised it's taken us so long to get here."

"Honestly, El? We didn't want to pressure you. There was so much going on with you, and what happened with Ainsley was complicated. None of us wanted to pressure you into *another* change."

We step into the refreshing cool air of the restaurant. Taryn's words sink in and I wonder if there are any other times I've been the reason Ainsley has been excluded. Taryn only gets so few hours off work and this is the first time Ainsley has joined us. It actually makes me feel bad to know that they may not have been spending time together because of me.

I hang back while Taryn greets the hostess, an old work friend. I pull out my phone and fire off a text to Charlie, questioning if this really was a good idea. I know it's my insecurity making me feel wishy-washy, but that doesn't mean it's easy to conquer. I want Ainsley to like me. I don't want her to judge me for what happened with Charlie after the gala. It was this need to be liked, to be the girl that fit in Charlie's world, that drove us apart in the first place, and I won't stand for it again. Before I can spiral further, the door opening catches my attention.

"Elia?" Ainsley asks, stepping inside.

"Hey, Ainsley," I say, trying to inject cheer into my voice. I wince alongside her at the fakeness of my voice. I wish I could get a rewind button and start over.

"Elia, you really don't have to do this," she offers, and I shake my head.

"I do. You did nothing wrong, and making you the villain isn't going to solve anything. So let's just. Let's try and start with a somewhat clean slate." I hold my hand out to her. "I'm Elia."

She looks at my hand questioningly, then shakes it. "I'm Ainsley." She gives me a small, tentative smile, which I return with a big, cheesy one. There really isn't getting over the awkwardness of the situation, so I try to find some sort of common ground that won't land us in trouble.

"I have to ask, did Charlie always leave his wet towels on the floor when he was with you or is that a new habit?"

Ainsley's eyes pop for a moment, big and wide at the mention of the shared history with Charlie, and I wonder if I swung too wide on it. Honestly, though? Ignoring that they were together would be so, so much worse, but Ainsley just laughs.

"The man is incapable of hanging a towel up to dry after using it."

Our laughter catches, and I know that Vivian is right and we will be great friends.

Vivian is the last to arrive, but Ainsley and I are already chatting about her hair. She's got her blonde locks braided into a crown around her head, giving her a youthful look. I've never had the patience for braiding my hair, so I love to see how other people are able to do it.

"I haven't decided if I want my hair up or down for the wedding, but this design is super cute," I say admiringly as she twists her head so I can look at the back.

"Have you decided what kind of wedding you're having?" she asks, and I wonder if this is weird for her. She's no doubt heard Vivian wax poetic about all the wedding-associated tasks she seems to come up with. I love Viv, but when it comes to my wedding she keeps creating more things for her to-do list, like what thickness cardstock I want for the programs so she can negotiate a bulk deal with the printer for the invitations.

"Sorry, sorry I'm late!" Vivian announces, dropping into her seat. She pushes her dark hair back. It's Sunday Funday, so I'm surprised to see she has her laptop case over her shoulder.

"Everything alright?" Taryn asks, sipping her mimosa.

"Yeah, just, this stupid file. It's fine, I'm here, and perpetually cursing Knox Benedict. I'm here for the mimosas."

"I'll drink to that," Ainsley says, lifting her drink.

"So, what? Were we talking about the wedding?" Vivian asks after downing her drink. She catches the waitress' eye as she starts toward our table. To save her the steps, Vivian gestures with her glass and a wink.

"Yes," I say with a heavy sigh. It feels like every reminder of the wedding is just another reminder of all those who won't be there. Whenever Charlie and I discussed what our guest list would look like, he always had so many names. College friends, fraternity buddies, business colleagues. Then he had extended family to account for as well. The whole situation got more and more daunting. Charlie has so many people he would want to invite, but my list is so small. When we first started to think about what size wedding we wanted, each of us made a list of everyone we would invite. Mine capped out at ten, while he had over a hundred without including business contacts his mother and stepfather would want. Charlie has helped me get better acquainted with some of his other friends, namely Walt, a prep-school friend who is going to be officiating the wedding, and one of his friends from college, Chad, who is everything you would expect from a Chad.

"Still got those guest list blues?" Taryn asks, twisting her lips into an apologetic frown. Calling them blues is an oversimplification of the problem.

I glance at Ainsley, who seems open to the whole conversation. I wonder if there are any lingering feelings over planning my wedding and not hers.

She seems to read my mind. "If you think this is weird for me, it's not. But I do wonder if you're inviting Uncle Hulbert."

My hand hesitates when I reach for my drink. "Probably not, since I haven't met him. But we're planning to keep it small, just immediate family and good friends."

When it was obvious the wedding would be a bit one-sided, Charlie suggested keeping it small and intimate. I took it one step further, suggesting that we return to Bora Bora, the place that really sparked our relationship.

"Count yourself lucky. Hulbert was...handsy." Ainsley shudders and takes a big sip of her drink.

Part of my mind hisses in jealousy at her being so well acquainted, but she and Charlie had years together. It's not unusual for her to know more people than me.

"Have you picked a location?" Taryn pushes after our food is delivered.

"Actually, tell me more about this Knox," Ainsley says. Catching my gaze across the table, she gives me a little wink. I'm glad to have the attention off me and the wedding plans.

Vivian thankfully takes the bait. "Oh, don't get me started on Knox. This prick calls me at, like, noon on *my* summer Friday, and says that he's away for the weekend but needs to hammer out details on the contract and if we don't have terms and a rough version of the contract by Monday at nine a.m., his client is going to walk away from the deal. This after he spent the entire week dodging my calls. So I got to go into work today to hammer out this deal."

"To men," Taryn says, raising her glass. "Can't live with them, and murder is illegal in all fifty states. Not to mention, we need men for orgasms, so we're stuck with them."

We cheers, but Ainsley shakes her head. "That's categorically false. I get off just as well, if not better, with my vibrator, and there's less cleanup, I don't have to negotiate with it about wearing a condom or if it's been tested, and I don't have to worry if I hurt its feelings when I get things started but change my mind."

"Guys, I haven't orgasmed since before I started this job," Taryn says. "And even then, it was like two months before that since Brad made me orgasm."

"I thought you stopped sleeping with him?" I ask.

"I did, and then I didn't, and then I did again, but I'm so busy and sometimes it's worth having a sure thing. You know my life. Between school and work, I had no free time to try to find someone else to sleep with. So I stick with what works, even if the Cowboys have a better win average than I have orgasms."

"Can I get an amen?" Vivian asks miserably into her drink.

"I feel like I should sit down and shut up," I say with a laugh.

"Do not be sorry because you are getting steady dick," Ainsley says more to her fifth mimosa than me.

"Good steady dick too," Taryn says with a laugh.

"You're making this weird, guys..." I warn, but can't stop the smile from spreading on my face. I hit the lottery with Charlie and I know it.

"Am I the only one who hasn't slept with Charlie?" Vivian asks, looking around the table at the three of us.

Ainsley flags down the waitress for another round. "Yep, this is definitely weird," she mutters.

It should be awkward, sharing drinks with two women who used to sleep with my fiancé, but it makes me feel oddly comforted. They're both incredibly beautiful women who are whip-smart and funny. They have all the hallmarks of perfect partners, yet Charlie picked me, a mess of a woman who doesn't know which way is up on a good day.

Ainsley must see the contemplation on my face because she gives me a grin. "It was only ever going to be you, Elia. He was wasting his time with us until you could be in his life."

Something about this statement, about the open, raw honesty on her face makes me reach forward and grab her hand under the table.

If Charlie loved her once, I know I will someday.

Three

⁓

VIVIAN - ONE MONTH LATER

I'M glad we splurged on first class. Taryn had been hesitant, and I don't blame her. I helped her work out a budget with all her loans and rent, and it's not pretty. She's smart and has a penchant for numbers, but she admitted to getting a sort of paralysis every time she looked at it. And I get it, really I do. There is something daunting about six-figure debt.

When it came to putting down money for this trip, I told everyone that I would charge it to my card and we could sort it all out later. The truth is, there will be no sorting it out later because Charlie has been letting me charge every step of this trip to his black card. He slipped it to me one night while watching Mr. Eligible when Elia was in the bathroom and told me to spare no expense. And I would have spared no expense, but we're being cloak and dagger about it because there is no way Elia would have let this happen. So I'm pretending I'm tracking who owes what and how much everything is costing and after the trip, I'll promise to give everyone their final totals, but conveniently forget until everyone has let the fact that there is money due fade from memory. I'll pretend like the room was upgraded for free or dinner was comped.

It's a small fib that some part of me feels bad about, but I don't want Elia to worry about it. I want to focus on really putting everything that happened behind us. There are moments, small ones, where she'll offer to make me coffee and ask if I still like it loaded with milk, and my option is to lie or watch the hurt cross her face when I tell her I drink it black now. I'd rather spare my friend these little pains if I can. She's been through so much already.

Elia is passed out beside me, her eye mask covering her face. Her life since she met Charlie has been something from the movies. First class flights, penthouse apartments and her photo on page six. It is certainly a bigger life than she ever bargained for, but she's taken it in stride.

Just like how she's taken adding Ainsley to our hangouts now. I wasn't sure how Elia would react when I floated the idea, but she jumped in with both feet. It was such a tremendous relief knowing that these two parts of my life could finally connect. I know Taryn was just as relieved. It's so much more than just wanting the ease of having the two of them hang out; it's that these two women I love are finally connecting.

Ainsley was the one who talked us into the first flight out of JFK. She argued that we could just sleep on the plane and arrive fresh and energized. Except I'm a shit flier, and I'm trying to deal with reviewing loan documents before I log offline totally for the weekend. My anxiety over wanting this weekend to go perfectly has me in its thrall.

Society has made it unacceptable to have anything wrong with you, that recognizing that there is a slight chemical imbalance or emotional response somehow makes you less than.

I have anxiety and I know there is nothing wrong with that, but I need to keep a clear head. I need to stay focused on getting these documents out to Knox fucking Benedict and keeping the mood light and airy for my friend, even if it means that sometimes my head feels light and I want to pass out. Therapy is probably the right next step, but carving out time for something I'm managing doesn't feel like a priority.

The flight attendant passes by again and checks to see if I want another mimosa. I'm tempted to change my order to a screwdriver, hold the orange juice, but this weekend isn't about me, it's about Elia. It's about making sure she has an amazing time and makes new memories to replace the ones she lost.

When we get off the plane, everyone looks so much more relaxed than I feel and I'm a little jealous. I feel more frazzled as I check my phone to make sure our ride is here. The text confirming that the driver is waiting by the baggage claim is worth a momentary relaxation. When we finally emerge to the level with the ground transportation, I beam at the limo attendant who holds a tablet with the words "ELIA'S BITY BACH PARTY" on it.

My molar might crack from how hard I'm grinding my teeth. It was supposed to say "Bitchy Bach" and if that was a problem they *should* have told me ahead of time. I also requested he have a penis balloon, but all he has is a solitary pink one. Not the grand welcome I was hoping for, but it will do. Plastering on what I call my pageant smile, I grin at Elia as I reach into my oversized purse and pull out the tiara and sash I've been lugging around. Thankfully, the cheap plastic did not snap while under my seat or as I went through security.

"IT IS TIME TO PARTY!" I shout as I crown her. She laughs, fixing the tiara so it's not caught in her hair. Taryn grabs Elia's bag so Ainsley can slip the sash over her shoulders.

I check the itinerary as the bored driver loads our luggage into the back of the limo. Elia doesn't know the difference, but I had requested the hot pink hummer limo so she could stand in the back and look out the sky roof as we drove down the Strip. Everything I have been trying to do is to make up for the last five years we missed together.

"Everything okay?" Ainsley asks, hanging back.

"Besides that being the limo I ordered?" I whisper, pointing at a group of shrieking bachelorettes just a little bit down from us who are piling into a hot pink hummer with a sky roof. There are fourteen of them and most of them were on our plane. They were not in first class, but I could hear their chattering the whole flight. I'm not saying they're the reason for my bad mood, but I'm not *not* saying that either. It's perfectly plausible that they used a different company, perhaps one more reliable, since as far as I'm concerned, this is now strike three. It helps to have someone else I can direct my ire at.

This is not for me, this is for Elia becomes my mantra, because it has to be my mantra. All these minor irritations are my own problem, not hers. She's currently taking selfies with Taryn in front of the limo with a huge grin on her face. Elia doesn't know the difference, so if things aren't perfect I get to be the only one who is the wiser.

"This is awesome. What else is stressing you? We've lived together for long enough that I know the 'Vivian is stressing' face. I can practically see the anime forehead flare on your face."

"I do not..." It's pointless to argue with Ainsley. She's been sitting at the table, helping me plan this, listening to me argue with the hotel over needing to get into the room early to set up. It's why I wound up booking the hotel room a night early, so I would be able to get in this morning and set up. Only I can't mysteriously go missing and if the hotel had only agreed to decorate for me, this wouldn't be a fucking problem.

"Viv!" Elia shouts, pulling me from my downward spiral. "Come take pictures!"

I flash my fakest biggest smile. "Coming!"

Ainsley and I move back to the group and the grumpy driver finally relents, taking a photo of the four of us with my phone.

Once we're inside the limo, I catch Ainsley palm the driver some money with a bright smile. I shoot her a questioning look, and she gestures, twirling her finger around. We may not get the sunroof standing I wanted, but we will get a nice tour of the Strip, I hope.

"So what's the plan?" Elia asks, popping the bottle of champagne. Calling this drink champagne is actually an insult to all the champagne pretenders out there. This is practically sweetened beer, but we all grin and pretend like we're enjoying it.

This company will definitely be getting an email from me about this. I try not to be a bitch about these things, but I'm not getting what I paid for.

"Well, we're going to get to our hotel and then I figured we could wander the Strip, maybe get some real breakfast. Really, this place is a nonstop party, so we could go to a topless pool and or a normal pool party." My brain is short-circuiting, realizing that I can't leave Elia alone while I go set up the room. Any one of us going missing will be way too conspicuous.

"Breakfast sounds great," Ainsley interrupts, saving me from my mental spiral. My phone vibrates in my hand and I open it, almost hoping it's a work email. I could always use that as an excuse, but I'm Elia's maid of honor, her best friend. I can't very well go missing. Why didn't this occur to me earlier?

You have panic face.

I do not have panic face, Ainsley.

Your panic face is so panicked that your eyebrows have developed the anime anger flare on them.

Sleep with one eye open tonight, bitch.

Ainsley sticks her tongue out at me.

Taryn catches my eye, looks between Ainsley and me, and cleverly turns to Elia. "Oh look! It's the New York, New York! We should go there and mock it for how familiar it is, like, 'Look at us, leaving NYC just to go to fake NYC in Vegas!'"

With Elia thoroughly distracted, I look at the new text.

Quit being a martyr and tell me what you need.

> A clone. I need a clone to set up the room while we hang out with Elia. If we had someone else coming or if I had thought about flying out a day earlier...

STOP. Trust me?

> More than I trust myself right now.

Then chill, I've got this.

"I forgot, which hotel are we staying at?" Ainsley asks, still scrolling through her phone.

"The Cosmo," I supply, glad to have an easy answer. Ainsley winks at me, turning back to her phone.

"Everything okay?" Elia asks, eyeing me and my phone. Maybe Taryn wasn't good enough at distracting her. It's like I can feel that giant sweat droplet on my brow telling her that I am most decidedly *not calm*. "Is it work? That Knox guy again?"

I practically sigh, grateful for the excuse she's handed me. "Yeah, loan docs. I finished my mark-up but won't send them to him yet, because I know he's just going to be an asshole and follow up again."

"And I just swiped right on a little coast-to-coast hookup. Don't mind me if I disappear for a bit." Ainsley says with a grin.

"Is going a weekend without a hookup too much, Ainsley?" Taryn teases, raising an eyebrow.

"Why? Jealous?" Ainsley asks, knocking back her drink.

"Nope, just want to make sure you know that this weekend isn't about your insatiable libido."

"I'm well aware that this weekend is for Elia. I may be a last-minute invitee, but that doesn't mean I'm oblivious. What, did you sleep on the wrong side of the bed?" Ainsley's tone has a hard edge though her smile is serene.

Taryn is right, but she doesn't realize that this is Ainsley helping me. At least, I think it is. No, I have more faith in Ainsley than that.

"Maybe you can both take it down several notches. If anyone other than Elia wants to fuck this weekend, then just get fucked, literally."

"With my full support," Elia adds with a laugh. There is a forced edge to it, and my worry rises. I know how Elia is with weekends like this. She won't speak up if she's upset, desperate to keep the peace. It's how she wound up having to share a bed with one of the Zeta pledges during spring break sophomore year. Every morning, she and I would sit on the balcony, talking about if she should do something about the morning wood that would wake her after they wound up spooning in the middle of the night. I should have done the better thing as her best friend and had her share the bed with my boyfriend and I, but it was too entertaining otherwise.

Thankfully, the awkward silence doesn't last long after Taryn starts in about the last time she was in Vegas, and we're able to swap stories until we get to the hotel.

"So I wasn't kidding about the hookup," Ainsley says. "I'll take our stuff upstairs, and connect with you guys after I connect with my inner goddess."

I mouth her a *thank you* before we lead Elia onto the Strip. I lag behind where Elia and Taryn are walking arm-in-arm so I can text Ainsley what to do. Setting up for a bachelorette party is self-explanatory enough that I'm not stressed, but not being there to oversee it is pulling at me. While Elia is distracted, I text Ainsley with all the things that are in the room and how they should be set up, including the screenshots I grabbed of decor ideas.

Fortunately, Elia has no shortage of things she wants to see on the Strip. We check out the Fountain at the Bellagio and stroll through the Venetian.

I feel like a double agent, texting Ainsley every fifteen minutes to ask how it's going. The last text I get from her is a middle finger emoji and a warning: "Much faster if you left me the fuck alone."

We're in a high end boutique, convincing Elia to try on a party dress for the club we have bottle service at for the next night, when Ainsley finally connects with the group again. Her pretty lips are twisted into a self-satisfied grin.

"That is the look of a well-pleased woman," Taryn teases, spinning in her own scarlet red dress.

"Yes, I am," Ainsley tells me with a wink. My heart swells, knowing that her satisfaction is from being able to do something nice for me and for Elia.

"Well, I have a surprise that is going to make satisfied women out of all of us," Taryn says with a grin.

My body goes rigid, but I plaster a smile on my face. "Surprise?" I manage to squeak. Elia glances at me in the mirror. I clear my throat and adjust my tone. "Surprise?"

"Yes, I noticed we had a window in our plans and I went ahead and made us reservations, so we should go ahead and check out if we want to make it in time!"

Four

AINSLEY

THE ROOM DECORATING wound up being a lot more fun than I expected. As Vivian hoped, there was a bundle of balloons at the check-in desk, including a penis-shaped one that the hotel clerk apologized to me for having to cover with a black garbage bag. It's pretty cheesy, the whole outfit, but I think it will work. There were a few struggles with setting up a banner, but I lucked out when I poked my head into the hallway and found a bachelor party setting out for the day. All it took was a pretty smile and the bat of my eyes and I was able to get a few of them to come in and help me finish not just decorating, but setting myself up for what should be a fun weekend of drinks and hookups.

I think I can see Vivian's eye twitch as Taryn starts to herald us out of the shops. Both she and Elia got gorgeous show-stopping numbers for the club we're going to tomorrow night. Taryn offered to pay for Elia's white dress alongside her own red one, but Elia beat her to the punch. It's not a secret that Taryn is working her ass off at a restaurant during the semester to help cover her bills. She has tenacity like no other, but this weekend is just an added expense.

"What are you doing?" I hiss, looping my arm into Taryn's and holding her back behind Elia and Vivian.

She looks surprised. "I'm taking us to a spa because I'm pretty sure Vivian's anxiety is going to turn her hair white before the end of tonight, and you decided to go off and screw some rando instead of partaking in this girls' weekend."

"Wow, bitch much?" My words are more of a snap than I expected, but I don't feel bad about it. She's been sort of an asshole about me hooking up, and I'm tired of it. She's never been like this before, even when we were in college. During the times when Charlie and I were off, I was dating around and it was a not incorrect joke that I was dating his fraternity. I like sex. I like getting off and knowing the power I have over men when they want me. I like it all, and if that makes me a slut or a ho or whatever other derogatory term men have come up with for a woman that likes sex, then so be it. But never would I expect to be shamed by Taryn. It's why I've been hesitant to talk more deeply about my relationship goals with my friends. I've written myself into the wild-child friend category, and I worry they won't take me seriously. Rather than potentially confront that, I chose not to even broach the subject.

I don't think they would look down on me, but there is this societal belief that a woman should want a monogamous relationship, and I do want that, but I also want to have fun and get laid because the guy chatting with me on the dating app I'm on has a rocking bod and is a yoga instructor. Why can't a woman want both things without being called a slut?

Taryn opens her mouth to say something, probably equally bitchy, but then her entire posture deflates. "You're right. That was bitchy and really undeserved. You know I have no problem with you sleeping with whoever you want."

"Then why are you suddenly the chastity police?"

Taryn's steps falter. "Because...I'm wondering if I made the wrong decision. Business school feels like such a waste of money and I hated my internship and my hours. I was working twenty to

twenty-two hours a day because no one wanted to take me seriously. I was asked to do all the bitch work, which, fine, I was an
intern. But what, I'm supposed to work like I have no life and
pretend this is what I really want? Is the paycheck enough for me
to go through this?

"My professors don't care, my classmates, the male ones
anyway, say that I'll make a nice desk ornament because that's all
I'll ever be good for, looking pretty sitting on their desks, not able
to contribute anything worthwhile to any company I'm a part of."

"Do you want advice or just to have a friendly ear?" None of
that explains why she's on my case in particular, but that can come
later.

Taryn seems to consider this. "I just want a friendly ear. I'm in
too deep. It would be like you deciding during 3L that you didn't
want to be a lawyer."

"Taryn, I did decide during 3L that I didn't want to be a
lawyer. I had that awful internship with that prick who tried to
convince me that we were doing the Lord's work protecting an oil
company from sanctions after a spill. I wasn't going to give up all
that work, so I went with being a mediator instead of going into
big law. You just need to find what works for you."

"Except that I can't. I'm drowning in undergrad and business
school loans."

"You know I'm always happy to help any way that I can."

"Unless you have a spare half million laying around, I don't
think you can."

"Your loans are that bad?" I was lucky; my father had the
money to cover all my schooling. I know loans can be killer, but I
never really thought about it. There is a reason they call it a
student loan crisis.

"They're that bad."

Taryn's voice is flat. She's well-educated and her salary before
business school was a lot, but New York City is expensive. I can't
even begin to imagine the stress that other people might be under.

32

Vivian and Elia come to a stop and turn to face us. Taryn and I are so engrossed in our conversation that we collide with our friends. It's a trip to watch the tightly controlled effort on Vivian's face as she zeroes in on Taryn.

"I don't know where we are going," Vivian points out tersely. Her lips are pressed into a thin line as she breathes through her nose.

Taryn doesn't back down. "That's right, so why don't you settle in, and relax?"

Vivian looks like someone you don't casually tell to relax. The breath Vivian takes to calm herself is audible, but no one says anything, least of all Elia, who bites on her lower lip. Viv's eyes might actually flash red.

"Don't try your luck," Vivian warns with an edge to her voice before she catches herself again. "Save it for the casino."

The surprise Taryn leads us to is amazing. She managed to book us a group massage and facials. After she checks us in and the woman is explaining the offerings, I step back to the front desk and swap out the credit card used to reserve our spot. I love Taryn and I love her for doing this, but based on our conversation, I'm not going to let her drive herself further into debt when I can help. We're also going to total out at the end of the weekend, and I'll let Vivian know that I'll help cover Taryn's share. I can't cover the whole thing because I know she'll flip about that, but I'm going to help where I can.

After changing into a robe, I'm led into a room where I'll be getting a joint massage. Since the location isn't really set up for group massages, the best they can do is pair us up in the couple's rooms. I'm surprised when it's Elia on the other side.

"Hey!" I say, hoping not to startle her. It doesn't work and she jumps, turning to face me and sliding her phone into her pocket. She looks guilty about something, but I'm not sure what.

"Hey!" she responds with equal cheer.

"Is this weird for you? I feel like I was thrust upon you for your weekend."

"Probably about as weird as it is for you to be at the bachelorette party for your ex-fiancé's new fiancé."

"It is a little incestuous." This gets a chuckle out of her.

"It's really okay that you're here. I need to rebuild my friend circle, but it's sort of hard doing that as an adult. Like, everyone is already established and you mostly make new friends in the office or at work, and I don't have that. I could get a job and Charlie would be totally okay with that, but at the same time, I like my world small. I like having the handful of people I know and trust. It's stupid, but it feels like if I only have people in my life vetted by the ones I love, I can't get hurt again."

My heart goes out to her. We never talked about what happened when she came back from her ex's, crashing back into Charlie's life the same way she did the first time, hurt and alone. I was there to see the fresh bruises on her neck and face and the pain in Charlie's eyes from not having protected her from this better. But I'm not one of her confidants, so we've never openly discussed it. This is the closest we've come.

"You know Charlie will never let anyone hurt you again."

Elia waves me off. "I know that. I'm just being needlessly emotional." She's fidgeting, pulling the tie around her robe tighter.

"Permission to speak freely?"

Elia's eyes snap to mine, and she nods.

"You went through something incredibly traumatic. You are not going to dust off your shoulders and get going like nothing happened. You need to heal from everything that occurred with your ex. You need to heal from the accident and I don't mean physically. You have so much that you need to work on that it's going to take time. Your ability to bury the hatchet with me is something that is incredible."

"You say that like you're some boogeyman." Elia gives me a weak smile.

"No, but I wouldn't be cool hanging out with my guy's ex the way you are. Especially not after what went down. I get it, Charlie is worth it ten times over, and I couldn't be happier for both of you. I know what he sees in you. You're kind and generous and selfless. You look for the good in people and that has burned you, but you shouldn't let it ruin your outlook on life."

Elia appears to be mulling this over when there is a light knock on the door, signaling our massage therapists' arrival. Quickly, Elia wipes her eyes and calls for them to enter, ending our conversation. I want to go to her and hug her, but we're instructed to lie on the table, and nothing more passes between us. I only hope I haven't said the wrong thing.

Five

TARYN

VIVIAN IS furious with me over the massages and refuses to say as much. I try to feel bad for her, but I can't find it in me. We're all exhausted, overworked and mad about one thing or another. We *need* to relax before there are true crime podcasts about this weekend. Not that Elia would be instigating, but she would try to get into the middle to break us up and end up dead as a doornail as we all bleed out from the wounds we would give each other. There is so much going on in each of our lives that's just magnifying our stress tenfold, and it's making us all irritable. A misogynist would be asking if we were all on that time of the month.

I let those ridiculous thoughts out with a heavy breath, instead focusing on the fingers diving deep into my back. I need this. Was it an absolutely absurd price to throw down for what amounts to two hours of time? Totally, but I can't regret it now. Not as my breathing deepens and I let my mind slip off to sleep while the massage therapist works away the mistakes of my internship.

I never thought I would be happy to be back in business school, but I absolutely am. Logically, I know what happened during my internship was not my fault, but I can't help the shame that colors my cheeks when I think about it. I was played the fool, and I can only hope it doesn't ruin my reputation.

Halfway through my internship, I met with one of the partners I was working with, trying to make my case for why I should take the lead on a particular section. It was what I had done before I started at the firm and there was no reason I shouldn't be chosen over the other interns. I told the partner I was willing to go the extra mile for the chance.

We had two very different interpretations of what the extra mile meant. It's why I left his office early that night, shame-faced with the threat of being unemployable. I meant I was able to put in the hours, hours that I was already being crushed under, to ensure that it was done right. He thought I was better suited to helping the team, or at least him, from my knees.

Human resources had a very different opinion than him. The firm made overtures of extending a job offer for after business school much earlier than they did for any other intern, but I saw it for what exactly it was: a bribe. I'm not sure if it was meant to stop me from suing them or keep the whole event to myself. It didn't stop my entire team from finding out, especially after the partner was escorted out by security, screaming about "that lying bitch" while pointing a stubby finger at me.

The memories of it drag me from my peaceful state too early.

The massage is over much too fast, and the therapists leave Vivian and I to stir and re-robe before we are led to Elia and Ainsley. I'm trying to inhale as much of the expensive aromatherapy as I can, hoping that my ills can be cured with eucalyptus and lavender.

"I hate you," Vivian mumbles into the faceplate on the table.

"You don't," I tell her, sitting up, not caring as the sheet falls away from my chest.

"I do a little. This was an awesome idea, and I don't know why it didn't occur to me."

"Because you tried to do too much on your own," I say gently.

Vivian sits up, turning to me, hugging the sheet to her chest. "Only because I want this to be perfect."

"And it will be, but who gives a shit that our limo wasn't pink? We have so many awesome activities planned. I'm sure it's all going to pan out exactly as you want."

Vivian is quiet, pulling her knees up to her chest. "I let her down, Taryn. I should have seen Bryan for what he was when they first started dating. I mean, it was all right there, textbook abuse, and I missed it. I wrote her off. So *I* give a shit that the limo wasn't pink."

"Viv, you did everything that you could have. She didn't let you see what was happening. Have you talked to Elia about what happened?"

Vivian scoffs. "Not a chance. I'm not going to poke at what is probably one of the most traumatic experiences in her life and be like, 'I know it was super hard on you when your ex abused you, but what about my feelings?' No, when she's ready to talk about it, she'll come to me, but I'm not going to push her on it."

I grab for my robe to move to comfort her, but Vivian has already closed off this line of conversation. She rises to her feet, quickly pulling her own lush robe on, keeping her back to me. I wonder if she's talked to anyone about how she's feeling. Given how she so quickly shut me out, I'm going to guess not. It's clear she doesn't want to talk any more on the subject, so I'll have to get her to talk to me after this weekend. She wasn't wrong earlier; this weekend is about Elia.

Ainsley and Elia are seated in a private facial room with four chairs. They're both sipping cucumber and lemon water, looking relaxed, and I feel like I just made a major score. I'll worry about the credit card bill when it comes due.

"This was such an awesome surprise," Elia says brightly as one of the women works on layering a clay mask on her face.

"Just remember these happy feelings when there is a dude

thrusting his banana hammock in your face," Ainsley says with a laugh.

I'm about to close my eyes so my facial can begin when I see Elia's eyes pop open. "What now?"

We all chuckle, but don't answer her as the women applying our masks cluck at us to quiet down so they can set. I'm surprised when they start to buff our nails and paint them. I'm not sure what color they're going with. I can only hope that whoever asked for it said that those who aren't the bride are wearing red.

I nearly fall asleep as they massage my head again, and thoughts creep in that this might be too relaxing. Maybe I should have saved the massage for the last day.

Elia is teetering in her heels as she slams back another shot in our hotel room. Vivian is quick to thrust a lime in her mouth with a laugh. From the one New Year's Eve we spent together, I knew that Elia could drink, but this is a whole other level.

When we got into the room, all of us were so surprised, except for Ainsley, who shimmied her shoulders. I felt bad for the comments I made about her only being interested in only getting laid. When I apologized to her, she only grinned and asked why she couldn't do both.

Ainsley shudders after downing her shot. "Who wanted tequila?" she asks, sucking on her lime.

"That would be the Bitchy Bachelorette," Vivian says with a sly smile.

"Pretty sure the sign said 'Bity Bach,'" I tease.

"Is that a reference to my size or the size of the party?" Elia questions as she pours out the next round.

I'm the only one who doesn't grimace while taking the shot

and wonder if that could have anything to do with me taking shots every day before bed during my internship. Not the healthiest habit, but it got me to bed each night while spreadsheets and slides danced over my head.

"We're going to be late!" I call, checking the clock. We quickly scramble to finish another round of shots before we head out. Elia is not steady on her feet, so she's attached to one of us at any given time. The cheese plate we had was clearly not enough food for her, because the liquor has gone straight to her head. In the mirrored elevator, I study her in her glittery white dress, looking the angel beside her squad of devils ready to corrupt the bride before her trip down the aisle.

In Vegas where bachelorette parties are a dime a dozen, she doesn't get any extra attention, which is not even remotely a problem. Elia doesn't seem to want it as her eyes catch on all the bright, shiny games and lights as we traverse our way to the taxi line. After only knowing her for a few months, it's hard to think that there was a time before we were friends. During the semester she and Charlie were out traveling the world, I stayed in their apartment to watch their two cats, Bonsai and Mochi. You wouldn't think it would make us closer, but it did. I offered to do it as a friend, but they promised to pay me since I was on the wrong side of Central Park from school. They called it taxi money, and while it felt weird to take it, I was grateful for the consideration.

The location the taxi is bringing us to is off the Strip. When Vivian asked me to look into fun locations we could take Elia that were on the more risqué side of things, I was happy to do research. This particular strip club operates on word of mouth, and it doesn't look like much from the outside.

When we pull up, I hand a blindfold to Elia, who raises an eyebrow. "Where are we?" she asks, glancing from the blindfold around to the rest of us.

"Put it on like a good girl, and you'll find out," I tell her with a laugh.

She blows out a puff of air and obliges, letting us lead her from the vehicle. The bouncer eyes us as we present our IDs. Ainsley is the one who adds a crisp bill to hers so he doesn't make Elia take off her blindfold.

"You here of your own consent?" the burly man asks Elia.

"For now, yes," she replies with a nervous laugh.

"I promise we're going to take it off in a few minutes," I assure her. And we will, once we're settled into our private room so our sexy cop/delivery guy/firefighter/plumber comes and shakes his ass in her face.

The music is throbbing and Elia is a good sport as we lead her into a room. It's a lushly decorated space with red velvet sofas and chandeliers hanging from the ceiling. My phone buzzes as we settle in and I pause, surprised by the text from Brad.

What are you doing tonight, baby?

I puzzle over how to respond before my thumbs fly over my keypad.

Wouldn't you like to know.

His response comes before I can tuck my phone away.

That is why I asked.

Not in New York, find someone else to booty call.

I tuck my phone away, relieved to see that I didn't miss much. A man walks into our room with a tray of shot glasses. He's shirtless and good-looking in a young prep school boy way. He's got richly tanned skin, which if I lived in Vegas, I'm sure I would too. Looking at him makes me feel older than the thirty-one years that I am. But who am I to judge? I would serve drinks at a strip club if it paid well and I didn't run the risk of having to serve my bosses.

"Hello, ladies, my name is Armando. These drinks are your welcome shots." He waits for us to each take one. Elia eyes it skeptically. "It's Goldschlager, compliments of the establishment," he assures us. We all cheers and then take the shot while Armando watches. "I'm going to be your waiter tonight. I'm going to take your drink orders and then I'll take your clothes off," he adds with a saucy wink.

Armando makes the pronouncement before he pulls off his tearaway pants. The music in the room cranks up to a volume that would blow out a normal person's eardrums, but Armando is unfazed as he goes straight to Elia, dancing and grinding.

She laughs nervously, trying to get into it, but she's plastered to the back of the chair, leaning farther and farther away as he grips the seat behind her and kneels over her.

"The bride-to-be isn't the only one with an itch to scratch!" Ainsley calls. I'm hoping Armando is taking the hint that he is not wanted over there as he moves to Ainsley, who greets him on her own two feet to dance with him.

A woman with a thong and tassels on her nipples enters with what I expect are our actual drink orders that we placed in advance. Elia nearly descends on the woman, grabbing a shot glass and pouring out the first thing she can get her hands on, which is vodka. She tosses it back like someone who does this on the regular.

Vivian and I share a look before looking back at our girl. Even Ainsley is shooting me a questioning look and I'm realizing that maybe an up-close-and-personal stripper is something we should have run past Elia.

"Are you okay?" Vivian asks her, beating me to the punch. Elia's hand is shaking as she pours another shot, this time with the bottle of tequila.

"Totes fine, just not drunk enough to have a nineteen year old thrusting his padded cock in my face." The second shot seems to soothe her ragged nerves.

The rest of the hour we have in the booth deteriorates. Elia wants nothing to do with the stripper, who doesn't seem to know what to do with a bride who is not trying to mount him. Elia actually asks if he has cards to play with, which confuses the poor boy. Every time he looks at her, she casts her attention elsewhere with the focus on refilling her drink.

He tries to get her to do body shots and she refuses, but when Ainsley suggests Elia do a body shot from her cleavage, she loosens up. The singles I painstakingly saved from Claudia Jean's get tucked into his hand and not his G-string when Vivian finally cuts him loose.

"I'm sorry, guys," Elia says, her words slurring.

"No! Not at all!" the three of us exclaim, jumping to assuage any misplaced guilt she has.

"We should have checked first," Vivian says, tucking her feet under her.

"The night is still young," I assure Elia, grabbing my phone. I see I have three texts from Brad. I'm not saying sleeping with my friend's fiancé's brother was a bad idea, but I'm not saying it was a good one either.

"Can I make a suggestion?" Ainsley asks from where she is lounging with the bottle of vodka on the floor beside her as she casually sips from her shot glass.

"Does it involve having a dick thrust in my face?" Elia asks.

I share a look with Vivian, mentally admitting how badly I fucked this one up.

"Not unless you want to. I can get us four tickets to a different strip show that is all fun watching from afar with zero touching."

"If you can promise no touching, I'm in. I'm not a total prude," Elia says.

"You owe zero explanation," Ainsley tells her fiercely.

By the time our hour is up, we have tickets for a show

tomorrow night before we go to the club. Vivian is probably taking the whole situation worse than Elia is, and I feel better watching them walk arm in arm down the Strip with their heads bent together. I take the moment to check my texts.

> I want to feel your wet pussy as you ride me like we're both going to die tomorrow.

> If you want me to make a trans-Atlantic booty call, all you have to do is ask.

> You give me blue balls when you play hard to get like this. When I see you again, I'm going to fuck you so hard, you're going to forget your own name.

The last text is accompanied by a photo of his hand wrapped around his cock, and I hate the thrill it gives me to know I have this effect on him. Still, I don't actually want anything more with Brad and should quit him like a bad habit. He's not even a particularly enjoyable bad habit. Fucking Brad is like what I imagine smoking feels like: being with him takes the edge off for just a little longer even though I don't particularly like him, but I can't get that fix anywhere else until I try a real relationship again, so I relapse. It might make me a bitch, but he knows that this is exactly what this is.

Elia throws her arm around Vivian's shoulder, her engagement ring glinting in the bright neon lights. The flare from the stone is like a shock to my system.

I don't just want to fuck around anymore. I want to find something like she and Charlie have, something that is real, and that is not with Brad.

> Magic 8 ball says 'Don't Count On It.'

VIVIAN

ELIA FEELS SO small under my arm as we wander through the endless shopping pavilions in search of a greasy burger. It seems like no matter which way you turn in Vegas, there is always some new way to separate you from your money.

"I *swear,* I am totally fine. Please stop worrying about it," Elia repeats for probably the hundredth time.

"I mean, if you insist, I believe you. I just. At Becca's twenty-first, you were the first one to grind up on the stripper. I never thought that it wouldn't be okay." I'm babbling. All of my hard planning for this weekend to be a success has been for nothing. I'm the reason it keeps crashing and burning. It's only the first night, and I've already made a colossal mistake, and I wonder how much else of this is also a mistake. I'm trying to bring my stress about it down, but I can't. I just keep seeing the distress on Elia's face as the guy hip-thrust into her face, shaking what his momma gave him.

I'm starting to spiral, questioning my every decision, when Elia laughs.

"Yeah, because I was sleeping with him at the time. He was some guy in my Intro to Philosophy class that I met with to study a few times, and we wound up banging. We were both super startled to see each other at the party. Oh, Vivvy, please don't worry about it. Once I have a burger and some fries and that special sauce, I'm sure we will rally tonight."

"Duh, there is nothing to rally because this is going to be an amazing weekend," I tell her, more for my own benefit than hers. I can only hope my voice doesn't betray the uncertainty I feel.

Taryn is the one to spot the burger joint we're looking for. It's crowded, so Ainsley and Taryn go to place the order, somehow sensing that Elia and I still need some time.

The moment a table opens up, Elia is practically leaping over people to claim it for us. I admire her dedication as she settles into the seat, proud of what she accomplished.

"Have you heard from Charlie?" I ask her, watching the rosy flush rise to her cheeks.

"Yeah, he said he was jealous that we took Friday off for the bachelorette. I might have texted him as we were getting the massages, saying how nice it was to not be working."

"Cruel," I admonish with a giggle. "When is his bachelor party?"

"No idea, and I don't think he knows either. He said Brad's been planning the whole thing. Honestly, I wouldn't be surprised if Brad just kidnapped him from work one day."

"I didn't realize they were close enough for Brad to be planning his bachelor party?" Everything I knew of Charlie and his younger brother, Brad, was that they were borderline estranged until Elia encouraged Charlie to invite his mother and brother over for Christmas Eve.

"Yeah," she clears her throat. "Brad offered to do it since Charlie didn't have a best man." Elia flushes again, but for a totally different reason.

It's the closest she's come to saying anything about Jack to me in months. I wish I had something to fidget with, but there is just Elia and I and this cavern of hurt between us. Jack should have been Charlie's best man. We should have been doing this whole thing twice, for my wedding and hers. The person I thought Jack was wasn't the person he proved himself to be. He manipulated Charlie, Elia and Ainsley like they were puppets on a string to keep me and Charlie away from Elia. He's the reason it feels like Elia's a million miles away sometimes. He's the reason I feel like I'm a million miles away sometimes.

This cavern between us is because of both of us, and we've been awkwardly dancing around, pretending everything is fine. That's not to say Charlie and Elia haven't been great about the whole thing, because they really have. They helped me move out and they gave me a place to get away when I wanted to be out of Ainsley's hair. I will forever be thankful for all the ways they have been there. We just never talk about it, about how I could be with someone who so clearly disregarded my feelings in attempting to do what he thought was right.

It's not the first time I've let this happen, that I've let myself be led astray by a man I thought loved me. Elia and I were already distant when Connor finally proposed, and her skipping my engagement party when she would have been the person to be my maid of honor stung. At the time, it felt like the final betrayal between us. I couldn't even count on her to be there for me during the good times, so there was no way I could count on her to be there during the bad. It's why after I caught Connor cheating on me, I crashed on a coworker's couch until I could get myself back on my feet instead of with Elia.

It feels so petty now. I should have known with how Elia was steadily isolated that something was up. It was because of my own selfishness that I missed all the signs.

"Viv?" Elia asks, squeezing my hand in a tone indicating it's not the first time she's said my name. Her touch pulls me back into the present.

"Yes?"

"Are you okay?"

"Absolutely."

Elia chews on her lower lip. "We can discuss this when we're back in New York, but I think you and Charlie need to talk about what happened with Jack. I think you're both carrying around a lot of misplaced guilt and I think you two could help each other move past it."

"When did you get so smart?" I ask.

Her eyes track over my shoulder, I assume to watch Taryn and Ainsley creep closer to where we sit now. "Not me, my therapist, but like I said, this can hold a week. It's held long enough."

"Animals! They're all drunken animals!" Ainsley shouts over her shoulder, nearly throwing the tray on our table. Taryn is behind her, holding a tray with four sodas.

"What did we miss?" I ask as we hand off each other's orders. Elia barely waits before shoveling nearly the whole burger into her mouth.

"Apparently animals are over here too," Ainsley muses with a laugh. "Some guy was high as shit and when our order first came out, he just grabbed a handful of the fries and shoved them into his mouth, not unlike Elia is doing."

Elia's eyes lift to Ainsley and she glares, snatching a cheese-covered fry off Ainsley's plate. Ainsley laughs at her, stealing a plain fry from Elia's plate.

"So, I got a job offer from the firm I worked with over the summer," Taryn announces, taking a long slurp from her soda.

"That's awesome!" We each congratulate her.

"I'm not sure I'm going to take it. I might try and leverage it for a better offer at a different location."

"Any particular reason?" I ask, knowing that she really needs a job with a good salary. For the three months she worked there, she earned the salary she would have had she not been an intern. I worked with her on a budget that would honor her desire to build some savings and pay off the school loans she and her parents took out for her education.

"I mean, I never saw the sun unless I was in a conference room that had windows. I think that's reason enough. I know that's what the industry is, and I know I have to work hard at it, but some guy on the team had to miss his sister's wedding because he got caught in a meeting and missed his flight. I don't want that life. I want to be here for weddings and babies and whatever life events come our way. I don't live to work, you know?"

"And we want you there for them," I assure her, squeezing her arm.

Ainsley opens her mouth, then freezes completely as she stares out at something. Taryn reaches over and closes Ainsley's mouth, bringing her back to focus. "We should get our fortunes told! See how much money Taryn is going to come into and how much amazing dick I'm going to get, and maybe how Vivian will hit some jackpot this weekend, because surely being that unlucky in love means you should be lucky elsewhere."

I scowl. "Haha, so funny, bitch. You're *hilarious.*" My tone indicates I think that Ainsley is in fact *not* hilarious. This is another deviation from the plan, but after what happened with the strip-per, I just need to let it go.

"I think it will be fun for you guys, but I have everything I need. I don't need a fortune teller to convince me I've met the love of my life. I'm sure every bride gets the same spiel," Elia says.

"If you're all going to be chicken shits, I'll go alone," Ainsley taunts.

"I didn't say I wasn't interested," Taryn says. "I am. Maybe the cards can tell me if I'm making the right or wrong call to turn down this job."

"Fifty bucks says that she's going to tell all of us we're going to fall in love and have babies, including Elia," I declare, knowing this is the easiest money I'll make. It's not a secret that Elia is not inter-ested in motherhood. She's perfectly content to have babies of the fur kind.

"I'll switch dresses with Elia," Ainsley volunteers. "That way we can see just how full of shit they are. If they can call that I am not the bride-to-be, then Vivian, you have to, hmmmm, you have to sext that hottie you're working with. What's his name, Fort Arnold?"

I snort, but my blood heats at the thought of my adversary. "That would be Knox Benedict. And no, I'm not sexting a work colleague. I have boundaries."

We ponder our options. "Karaoke!" Elia exclaims. "You two need to duet."

"I can live with that." I grin, pulling out my phone to see if I can find a way to make that work. Maybe I can try a peace offering in the form of drinks one night? Taryn plucks my phone from my hands.

"No planning. It has to happen organically. Once we're done eating, we'll have Ainsley and Elia switch dresses and then go get our fortunes told."

We do exactly that, sending Elia and Ainsley into the bathroom to change dresses. Taryn slips away to get us those yard-long margaritas. The idea wasn't to go super hard tonight since I have tomorrow all planned out, but now I have to move our dinner reservation to get to the strip show Ainsley found on time. Elia will probably enjoy the strip show much more than what I had planned.

Some might call me Type A, but I just like to think that I'm a woman with a plan. A plan that I like to stay on course and suffer no deviations. These deviations are, of course, for the best. The massages helped to relax us all and calm tensions. The show tomorrow night will be a hit, if the reviews I'm looking at are any indication. I like to be prepared and I was somehow woefully unprepared for this trip. At every turn, I'm just getting it wrong.

Elia emerges, Ainsley's dress a touch too tight on her. The plunging illusion neckline accentuates her breasts. Her hair is pulled back, her chestnut locks woven into a braided crown on the top of her head. With every step, she pulls down on her dress, trying to make the length longer, which will never happen. Elia has an easy four inches on Ainsley and the dress was short to begin with.

Ainsley is now donning Elia's crown and sash, winking at people as she passes. Her blonde hair flows freely around her shoulders and she tosses it with a saunter. Elia's dress fits Ainsley better than the other way around. When Elia reaches out to take her drink from Taryn, I notice her hand is bare and grab it.

"Your ring!" I exclaim.

"Is safe. I'm not wearing the real thing this weekend anyway. I actually almost never wear the real thing. Charlie and I went and got a secondary ring so I don't have to fret over it being stolen." Ainsley chooses that moment to flash the ring, wiggling her fingers.

"How much is your ring even worth? Didn't you get it insured?" Taryn asks, staring at the spot on Elia's hand where her ring should be. If you weren't looking for it, you would miss the tan line around her finger.

"I have no idea if it's worth that much, but he got me a ludicrously expensive necklace for Christmas. It wouldn't surprise me if my ring could feed a small nation. Also, of course, it's insured. I just don't want to risk it, you know?"

"Are we doing this or are we going to disseminate the cost of Elia's entire jewelry collection?" Ainsley asks impatiently.

"Let's go." I gesture everyone forward.

The shop is tucked into a corner. I'm surprised Ainsley even saw it from where we were sitting. The only sign marking it as a business is the neon tarot card in the window over another neon sign declaring it open 24 hours. The shop is empty when we enter. It's dark, and I wonder if we've stepped into an elaborate serial killer trap. There are tapestries and dark fabric hanging from the ceiling, giving the impression of a circus tent. Whoever owns this place is leaning in hard to the stereotypes of clairvoyants. Shelves of crystals and skulls line the walls, inviting people to get close with their 'do not touch' signs that are likely never obeyed.

Do I believe that there are people who are in touch with the spirit realm? Maybe not as much as they would like us to believe, but there are enough people in the world and enough unexplained events and phenomena that could be attributed to it. Just like there are people who are good at math and science or English and history, I'm sure there are people skilled enough at reading a room.

At the very center is a table with a crystal ball and five chairs set around it. There is a small bookshelf with crystals that seem to glow, probably from some battery pack, alongside books lacking titles. I don't see anything else for sale or even a pricing guide. In a city where everything comes at a price, I'm wary. Generally, places without prices posted are those that are going to gouge you. I'd bet good money that the cost of each reading is revealed after assessing the wealth of a particular client.

"Ah, right on time, ladies," a small woman says, emerging from the back. I'm not sure what I expected, but a young twenty-something with purple hair wasn't it. With a deep maroon bodice over a forest green peasant top, she looks like she walked out of a renaissance faire booth. Her layered skirt is a rich royal blue that ties the whole look together, complete with a small pouch at her waist. This woman is an explosion of colors. When she marks the surprise on all of our faces, she grins. "What? Expecting an old crone? Grannie took the day off, something about a poker tournament she was going to win."

"What did you mean by right on time?" I ask skeptically. I don't like how she meets my gaze with her shrewd eyes. She's sizing me up, probably marking me for the suspicious type.

"I mean," she affects an Eastern European accent, "the cards told me of your arrival." She waves her hand over the table with dramatic finger wiggles, showing off the stacks of rings she has on each finger. We all take a step back when a deck of cards appears. The girl giggles at our expressions. "Take a seat. Who should I start with? The bride-to-be?" When she says this, she's looking at Elia. Then she looks at Ainsley expectantly.

Ainsley plops down first and we all follow suit. "What's your name?" Ainsley asks.

"Esmerelda," the girl answers, holding her hand out for Ainsley's. Gone is the accent. When Ainsley places her hand in the girl's, Esmerelda yanks it toward her, twisting Ainsley's hand this way and that, surveying it. She drags a dainty finger along Ainsley's palm.

"Actually?" Taryn asks, though she's the least likely of us to question someone with an unusual name.

The girl sighs. "No, but I wish. It's just Esme, but after that sparkly vampire movie, everyone asks if it's short for something, like they think they're *so* clever."

"Sounds exhausting," Elia says sympathetically.

Esme releases Ainsley's hand and then places the tarot deck in front of her, instructing her to split the deck. She asks Ainsley to do it again, and when there are three piles in front of her, Esme waves her hand. As Ainsley flips her cards over, Esme makes pensive noises.

"What kind of explanation do you want? The cliffnotes version or the in-depth one explaining each card and blah blah blah? I want to make sure I don't lose the skeptic over here." Esme winks at me.

Ainsley leans forward, resting her chin in her hand. "Let's go for the quick and dirty version."

"Alright. From your palm, I learned you have a fractured love line. You have had love in your life, just not the forever kind. I can promise the man that purchased that ring is not for you. The next man that you give yourself, and not just your body, to is the man who will fulfill your most secret of desires. Your hesitations around family shouldn't hold you back. Your bond with your family, both blood and found, is bound to only get stronger once you stop fighting those connections. Now, should I do the actual bride?"

Ainsley laughs at this while I roll my eyes at Esme's vague proclamations. "What makes you think I'm not the bride?"

"For starters?" Esme points at Elia. "She's the one with the tan line around her ring finger and she keeps reaching for it like she's missing something. You, on the other hand, keep tugging on it like you're itching to get it off. Also, both of your dresses fit you poorly. I'm guessing you switched dresses, hence why the real bride's dress isn't zipped all the way and shows a little more leg than she wanted, if how she tugs on it is any indication."

"With those skills of observation, you should work for the FBI, Sherlock," Taryn chuckles, slurping from her drink.

"I would, but something about not liking my past history of illegal substances. Turns out answering honestly on the polygraph can also cost you the job." Esme sighs like she's tired of the charade we tried. Turning to Taryn, she points. "You have a specific question you want to ask?"

Taryn eagerly nods while Esme resets the cards. "You two go change in the back room. I'll get started and wait to deliver my awesome knowledge until you get back."

Elia and Ainsley quickly move to switch dresses, I'm sure making them each more comfortable. While they're gone, Esme rises from her seat, her voluminous skirts moving with her as she ducks behind the counter and comes back with a small box.

"Before this is all over, I'll have a gift for you. You already don't want to accept, but I'm going to insist," she tells me before turning to Taryn and taking her hand.

"Do I get a gift?" Taryn asks.

Esme shakes her head. "Sorry, sweetness, but you're not the skeptic who wants to run me out of town. You have a question for me, so ask before the cards and let us see what your future holds. But, like, ask in your mind, not out loud. It makes this next part so much better." Whenever she says something dramatic she drops her voice and waves her hands in a way not dissimilar to a rum-loving pirate. It's a great act, and I'll be sure to leave a tip for the performance we're getting.

I can't pinpoint why I'm so hesitant to believe Esme. Part of it is because I don't want to believe that our actions are foretold. That means that I always abandon Elia when she needs me most and that Elia was supposed to fall into that asshole's clutches. I refuse to let that be the case, because if it's not, if everything isn't pre-written, that means there might be some other universe where we made different decisions and Elia was never hurt and she found her way to Charlie another way.

Esme and Taryn do the same song and dance with the cards, with a different configuration appearing. Esme hums to herself while reading them. The shifting of the beads in the doorway signals to Esme that Elia and Ainsley are back, prompting her to begin talking.

"You want to know about business decisions. It looks like you had to make a very difficult decision in the past surrounding your career that you're still conflicted about." Esme reaches out and pats Taryn's hand. "You made the right call. It wasn't easy, but in the long run, it is beneficial for the universe and the other women in your office."

Whatever Esme meant by that, it means something to Taryn. It's astounding to watch the tension visibly leave her body. "Okay," Taryn says uncertainly, blinking furiously.

"You want to know if you should take this job? Don't. It will lead you down a path of self-doubt instead of self-discovery. The better opportunity will come at a time when you least expect it and it will lead you to your soulmate."

"Thanks?" Taryn doesn't know what to make of that, but she leans back in her seat, waiting to see where this is going to go for Elia and I.

I sit up a little, expecting that I'll be next, but the violet-haired girl only shakes her head. "You're last, skeptic."

"So me?" Elia asks, perking up and giving Esme her hand. I try to pay attention as she shuffles her cards and surveys Elia's hand, but I keep finding my eyes drawn to the box on the table, wondering what's inside. Probably some sort of charm for fifty bucks a pop.

"Alright, Miss Bride-to-Be. It hasn't been an easy road leading to your Prince Charming, but now that you're with him, you're exactly where you need to be. Your love line is uninterrupted and runs the span of your hand. No children in your future, except those with claws. Your past is full of questions, but your present holds all the answers that you need. As for your future, you will have a long, happy life with your groom." She pauses for a second, her brow wrinkling. "I would also say red is an excellent choice for the weekend." Even Esme doesn't seem to know what she means by this and shrugs.

My eyes roll so hard into the back of my head that it nearly hurts. "How could you know she'll have pets?"

"Do you want me to give you all my secrets on the first date? That's not how this works." I stare her down, waiting for an explanation. Esme rolls her eyes and slouches. "Fine! Twist my arm why don't you, councilor? She already has at least a dozen scratches on her hands, arms and legs. My guess is at least two cats; they're too thin to be dog scratches. Most pet parents are not one and done. There tends to be a history."

"How did you know she's a lawyer?" Ainsley asks this time.

Esme swivels her attention. "That I won't explain, but thanks for the confirmation."

Elia looks over at me, then back to Esme. "Now do Vivian."

"Are you sure she's ready for it?" Esme asks, looking at me as she reshuffles her cards.

"No, but she doesn't have a choice. It's my bachelorette."

I sigh and offer my hands, following each of the directions provided by Esme. Her hands are cold as she grasps mine. She lightly trails a finger down the center of my palm, studying it closely, and I have to fight the shiver that runs down my spine. When she's done reading my palm, I split the tarot deck without prompting, having already watched my friends go through this.

Esme only smirks as she reviews the cards I've flipped, calculating what they are and what sort of shit she's going to pull from her ass for me.

"So, left to right, we have the Five of Cups, the Two of Swords reversed and The Lovers." I'm actually surprised I'm the first one to have The Lovers card come up, given how much she's talked about romance. "The Five of Cups tells me that you're stuck in the past over something. Whatever it is, you need to do what you can to move on. Have the conversation that needs having. With it holding you back, you're not able to live to your fullest, and you strike me as the type of woman for whom not being your best is unacceptable."

I frown. "Who doesn't have regrets?" I challenge.

"Vivian," Elia starts, but I glare at her.

"Okay, so," Esme points to the cards before her. "The Two of Swords means you're at a stalemate. My guess is because you're too stubborn and whatever you haven't moved past is holding you hostage. Once you address it, you'll be able to transition more easily to The Lovers. It's not always a literal card, but for you, it is. Your palm confirmed a twice interrupted love line. Twice you have found love only to lose it, but this next lover is your soulmate. He will be the father of your two children. Boom, drop the mic." Esme leans back in her seat, reaching for the box.

"Is this your next sales tactic?" I don't know why I'm being such a bitch, but my face is hot from everything Esme said. It's an uncomfortable truth being told that I'm holding myself back because of my refusal to have a conversation. I don't have to be clairvoyant to know that it's talking with Elia about what happened, but it's useless to drag us both through what happened again.

To Esme's credit she doesn't look smug. She opens the box, facing it to me. Inside there are three bracelets that look like the power beads I had when I was a kid. She doesn't hesitate to grab my wrist and slide a purple one on.

"You need this one first. Amethyst will help you heal your broken heart. And this stone," she points to one of the handful of pink ones on the bracelet, "is rhodonite, which will help you move past your stagnant cycle."

"Do we all get bracelets?" Elia asks, watching with curiosity.

"Nope, just your friend here. This second bracelet is for when you start to feel open to loving again. It's made of obsidian, citrine and kunzite. Obsidian so you feel worthy, kunzite to help you build a strong bond with whoever it is you decide to be open with and citrine to help spark joy."

"How will I know when to start wearing it?" I ask, rubbing at the one already on my wrist.

"You'll just know," she tells me impatiently before pulling out the last one. "Carnelian for passion, Rose Quartz to fill you with the love you know you deserve and moonstone for harmony when communication breaks down."

I wonder if I'll need these sooner than I thought. Not for romance, though, maybe there is something to Esme's assertion that I'm closed off. No, I think perhaps I should wear the moonstone to finally talk to Elia. Despite Esme's entire skit being about romance, there is more to my life. But maybe I do need to realize that I should put myself out there again.

"Well, that's a nifty little trick," Ainsley chirps, studying the two bracelets in the box.

I roll the stones of the bracelet on my wrist between my fingers and fight back the urge to make some sort of snarky comment and accept the so-called gift. I'm not ready for love, and I don't know if I ever will be. That's a lie, I will be, I just don't know if I *want* to open myself up to that heartbreak again. Could that be my future? Finding a man and falling in love?

What would happen if I just learned to let go? I've always been Type A. I've always had a strong need to control everything, but after Jack and I broke up, things changed. It was no longer just about being able to have a plan and know what's going to happen.

When I felt that loss of power and control, my heart would race and my head would feel light. It still happens from time to time, but I have too much else going on to add a new doctor or medication to think about. Maybe when work slows down I can consider it.

"How much do we owe you for your services?" I ask pertly.

"Fifty per reading," Esme says, producing a card reader from some pocket.

"Well then." Ainsley pulls out a credit card and hands it over. "Since this was my idea, it's my treat."

I refrain from comment but tip the woman generously anyway. She might be a charlatan, but she's at least very good at reading a room.

"Thank you," Elia says, shaking Esme's hand with a glint in her eyes. Esme holds tight to her hand for a moment. The psychic looks tense and I move to intercept the two of them, unsure of what she's doing to Elia.

"Bob-o wants you to know that he's proud of you, and he likes this chap," Esme says, before shaking her head. "Did that make sense to anyone?"

Elia clamps her free hand over her mouth before pulling out of Esme's grip. She remains silent and then I remember that she used to call her dad Bob-o as a joke, one that she never explained to me. She and her parents would always laugh and say it was something you had to be there for.

"Thank you again," Elia says with a tremor in her voice before grabbing her frozen margarita and taking a long pull on the straw as she leads us out.

"I'll accept an apology in the form of a wedding announcement, skeptic," Esme calls after me as the door shuts behind us.

Seven

AINSLEY

I GRAB my boobs as I roll over so I can have an even tan. We might be at a topless pool, but that doesn't mean I need my double D's flying around when I move.

After the psychic last night, we decided it might be best to go back to our room. Each of us was a little lost in our own heads after what Esme said. I know at least I was.

The next man I give myself to will give me what I truly desire. But what is that desire? Is it desire in the carnal sense? There are so many things my heart desires that I don't even know where to begin. I try to think of the things I've always wanted but never dared to ask for, like having someone dominate me in the bedroom or maybe even a non-gross threesome, one where each partner is invested, not just because one dude wants to bang two chicks at once.

Something tells me that it's not a sexual desire, though. The one thing I keep coming back to is that I want to be a mom. I'm not as committed to plans the way Vivian is, but I always saw the way my life was supposed to play out with Charlie. We would get married and have a year of newlywed bliss before we started to try for a family. We would start with one kid and go from there. I was an only child and Charlie wasn't close to his brother, but I wanted to have a house full of love and kids. I wanted my kids to have someone they could turn to that would understand what it was like being raised by me when they got older.

That dream, those desires, went out the window, and while I haven't been committed to finding Mr. Right, or Mr. Eligible as the show wants me to think, some part of me always looks at my dates and wonders what a kid would look like with our shared features. I'm all about a good orgasm, but maybe that's why I've been so quick to dismiss men I don't see as right. Maybe it's because I'm secretly searching for a different kind of daddy.

The truth is, I'm torn, and maybe the right partner would make me feel less pulled in opposite directions. I'm torn between wanting my cake and eating it too. I want the fun, exciting sex, the filthy fuck-your-mouth-and-make-you-beg-for-it-again kind, but I also want that feeling of being cherished and loved and having the same person I can come home to. It's desiring the same person that I can have all those things with.

For now, at least I can focus on getting good dick while I decide how I want to go about becoming a mom.

Those next steps are terrifying. I know what I want, and I know the general way to go about getting it. Penis in vagina, semen fertilizes an egg. But to do it alone, do I go to a sperm bank? Do I subtly screen my dates for good genetic code and let them come inside me?

It's a whole lot of thinking I need to do when I'm out of the Vegas sun.

For a $50 psychic, she delivered some hard truths and opened up a whole lot of uncomfortable lines of thinking. If I'm struggling through the introspection she inspired, I can't imagine what is going through Vivian's head, though I assume it's why she's so quiet.

For our full day in Vegas, we started it off right with brunch before hitting the pool. Vivian rented a private cabana for us at the hotel. All afternoon, we've had a steady influx of water, booze and snacks to make sure we don't get sun poisoning. We're being disgustingly responsible.

Elia laughs into her phone then tucks it into her purse before turning on to her back. It took some cajoling, but we convinced her that she should totally go topless. We took a "When in Rome" approach, and after her third margarita and a confirmation text from Charlie that he wants her out there living her best life, she relented.

"You know you don't need Charlie's permission to do anything, right?" I remind her gently as she unclasps the front of her top. Her hands still as she lifts her gaze to mine.

"I know." Then softly, "I know." She looks away, biting on her lower lip as she thinks and I wait for her to go on. "It's not a control thing. It's a partnership thing. It's a love thing. I communicate with my partner because while it is my body and Charlie reinforced that I could do what I wanted and felt comfortable with, I would be pretty mad if he just told me he was walking around with his dick out at a nudie beach without me there. I would want the consideration of him asking, so I gave it to him."

"Very well put. We just wanted to make sure—" Vivian starts.

"I get it. You're trying to make sure I keep healthy boundaries and that I don't feel like I'm being controlled. Trust me, I love you all and appreciate you, but Charlie is just as protective of me as you are and is not controlling."

"We believe you," Taryn adds.

We all know what a catch Charlie is. Our concern wasn't born of worry about him but wanting to make sure Elia feels loved and supported.

"So, what is the grand master plan tonight?" Elia asks, deftly changing the topic.

"Same answer as the last four times you asked," Taryn admonishes, looking up from her book. She slips her bookmark inside it before rising, her shoulders pulled back.

Elia pouts. "I just want to know what to be prepared for."

"Anything and everything, but no dicks in your face." This from Vivian, who has been emailing all day with her adversary.

"Do you trust us?" I ask, getting up to join Taryn, who is headed toward the water.

"Duh, but it doesn't mean I like being in the dark."

"Surprises can be fun, babes," I try to tell her, but she doesn't seem to want to hear it, so instead she lies back with her hat covering her face.

Elia seems to be relaxing into the party mood, but I think she's still a little wary after last night. It just means we need to make sure she's good and ready for tonight.

Before we leave for the night, we sit around with glasses of champagne on the couch in our hotel room.

"Never have I ever slept with Charlie," Vivian says, wincing at her best friend before laughing. Elia seems to take the joke well enough because her head tosses back, her dark curls shaking.

"That was low," Elia warns, taking her drink. Vivian must sense retribution, because she tries to slink back into the cushions.

"Never have I ever slept with a colleague!" Taryn practically shouts, jumping up on the couch like some washed-up action star.

It's my turn to scowl, taking a sip, but I'm surprised when Elia and Vivian follow suit.

"Whaaaaat?" I ask, drawing the word out.

"My high school job. I started dating one of the guys I worked with and when he pointed out how extra useful the back room was, let's just say, I was never bored when we were scheduled together," Elia explains sheepishly.

"It only counts for me because my law school boyfriend and I worked at the same firm for a few months. It's actually why we got back together," I say, taking an extra sip of my drink.

"I thought you were off and on with Charlie?" Vivian winces. "Sorry."

"No, I'm curious too," Elia says, leaning forward.

I take a deep breath. "I was off and on with Charlie and usually when I was off with him while in law school I was dating this guy Sean, who was, like, perfection in a man. But during one of those off times his now late wife snapped him up and told me if I so much as batted my eyes at Sean again, she was going to shove the entirety of Harvard's law library up my ass until I fully absorbed the meaning of abandoned property and possession under the law."

Taryn sinks back down to the couch. "That is so hardcore. She sounds like a psycho."

"No, she really wasn't. She knew that I was stringing Sean along because of Charlie. She loved Sean, but he was always going to come back to me because he couldn't have me. I had a lot of respect for her, and was at their wedding and there for Sean after she died."

"Wow, that is so awful," Elia says, leaning back.

Vivian glares at me for bringing down the room.

"Elia, don't you owe Vivian a brutal never have I ever?" I ask.

Elia sits back up. "Yes, never have I ever had sex while my roommate was in the room."

"Oh, fuck off," Vivian snaps, sipping her drink. "How was I supposed to know you were there! You said you left for the weekend!"

"Okay, wait, no, this needs an explanation. The rest of us have been laying our sexual exploits bare. It's your turn, Viv."

Vivian's head drops back and she finishes her drink before refilling it, killing the bottle. "I was sleeping with a guy on the football team, and he was all hammer and no finesse. He was built like a fucking tank. So he had a thing for fucking me against a wall. I *thought* my roommate was home with her parents for the weekend. How was I supposed to know she wasn't? So we come in, and he has my skirt around my waist already, and he's going to pound town until he finishes because it was always a race to finish with him and I *never* won. So he goes to go to the bathroom to clean up the condom, and then Elia throws back her blanket and—"

"And since I had to listen to this dude squeal like a pig as he came," Elia tells us, "I asked if she was fucking kidding me."

"So then I said, 'Nope, just getting fucked.'"

They both burst into the hysterical laughter of two people used to telling this story with each other. Whatever memories Elia may have lost, I'm glad she got to hold on to so much good.

"Well, we're all going to be fucked if we're late, so, to the face like proper ladies and let's go," I order as we all drain our glasses.

When we walk out, the bachelors who helped me set up the room are in a heated argument with some woman in the hall.

"Hey, lads," I say before realizing that there is some trouble cooking. The woman turns to face me, her blonde hair pulled back, revealing a splotchy red face. It's clear she's been crying given how swollen her eyes are, but it seems she's moved on to the anger stage of grief.

"Are you the blonde that fucked my fiancé?" she demands, striding over to me and slapping me.

I'm too shocked to block it, but when she rears up to hit me again, I catch her wrist, stopping her. "The first one was a freebie. I don't know who your fiancé is, but unless your name is tattooed on his forehead, you're taking your anger out on the wrong person. Try the asshole that stepped out on you." I point to the guy I did sleep with, who looks the least harried about the whole situation. "I slept with that one, so you're barking up the wrong blonde tree."

The woman looks from me to the guy who is being blocked by two of his groomsmen to the guy I did sleep with, who nods in confirmation. The woman deflates.

"I just don't know what to do," she tells me tearily.

"Can I be honest with you? I'm a divorce lawyer. If he's willing to cheat before you get married, that's a behavior that's not going to change with a ring. I'm going to guess that there were indiscretions that preceded this one, otherwise, you wouldn't be slapping the first blonde woman you saw who acknowledged your husband-to-be."

The woman sniffles and seems to take my advice when she pulls off her engagement ring. "I'm going straight to the pawn shop with this," she snarls.

"Good luck getting anything for it. It's fucking glue," he shouts back.

"Your honor, I rest my case," I mutter to no one in particular as I hustle the rest of us past this drama and into the elevator. Once we're free of them, I rub my cheek.

"Did that shit *actually* happen?" Taryn asks before we all burst out laughing.

I hope the woman learns a valuable lesson from today.

"Aren't you a mediator?" Elia asks. "If that's not a totally rude question."

"Not rude, it's true. But people take 'lawyer' so much more seriously because they see lawyers as adversarial. I'm not sure any of those people were particularly interested in having me explain that as a mediator, I'm a neutral third party helping the couple versus an attorney who just represents one party."

I go on to talk about some of the more interesting divorces I've mediated.

Thankfully, we get to the strip show with no further issues and we're led to our seats. Elia sits comfortably, sipping on a rum and coke while we wait for the pre-show to begin. I think that this will be much more her speed. She's laughing and cheering, throwing around the show money they gave everyone at the start to protect the strippers' actual tips. There is bumping and grinding, but also a plot regarding consent, which is a big hit with Elia. Those not interested in participating in the grinding get to watch a wild show complete with water sluicing over the bodies of these men with abs for days.

Our seats are up in the balcony, away from being directly involved in the action, which I figured would suit Elia better. We have an excellent view, and when the strippers make their way up to us, they seek out the willing participants, namely, Taryn and me.

During intermission, Vivian grabs my wrist. "Thank you for this incredible save. I feel like we were losing her on this trip."

We're standing at the bar ordering more drinks while Taryn and Elia drunkenly discuss the merits of the plotline.

"Of course. I'm glad they had four tickets available."

"How did you pull it off?" she asks, slipping a tip into the tip jar.

"Money moves mountains. All it took was one email to my credit card client relations team, and they took care of it."

"Ugh, this is going to be an expensive AF bachelorette."

I ignore her complaint and put down my credit card to pay for the drinks. I look away from her for one second to glance toward Taryn and Elia and barely catch her switching out the card I put down. It's a sleight of hand that would make a Vegas card dealer wary. I narrow my eyes, but Vivian looks away from me in the direction I was looking.

"About that," I say. "I know you're splitting the weekend between the three of us in order to pay for Elia too. Let me take on a little more. I hate seeing how stressed Taryn is, and it's not fair for her to have to struggle to pay for this weekend when I can just pay without a problem."

"First, she'll kill you if she hears you say that. Second, remember when I said Charlie offered to pay? Charlie paid. He told me to do whatever it took to get Elia to have a nice time on this trip. So the room, the flights, the dinners, everything has been on him. It's why I've said I'll just cover it. He gave me one of his credit cards." Guiltily, she holds my card out to me.

I pluck it from her fingers with my eyebrows raised. "Elia might kill him for this."

"You know Charlie. He's not even batting an eye at what this weekend is costing. Did you hear he's paying for everyone to go to the wedding? Villas and all. He just wants Elia to be happy. Whatever price tag that comes with, he'll pay it."

"The world does not deserve Charlie Breckenridge."

"No, but Elia does. It's really awesome to see him treat her so well. I mean, I saw some of the guys she dated before him, obviously not *that* guy, but no one has ever come close to Charlie."

"I imagine it would be hard to come close to a guy who takes you to Bora Bora after kissing you once."

"Ain't that the truth," Vivian confirms.

I look back in Elia's direction. She seems relaxed and carefree. I don't know Elia the way Vivian does, but it's easy to see why Charlie fell in love with her. The part of me that wondered what it was about her that finally got Charlie to work less is satisfied. She's bright and bubbly and brings with her zero tolerance for the whims of the wealthy.

I grew up in that world. My father worked long hours, so having a barely-there partner felt like it fit. I didn't demand better of Charlie. Instead, I cut and ran when I realized that wasn't the life I wanted, when I realized Charlie wasn't the one I wanted, and I chose to use his work schedule as an excuse for ending things.

It was hard in the year after, knowing that I had hurt him to protect myself, but my actions, regardless of how shitty I feel about them, were right. They were right for me, and seeing how he and Elia glow around each other, I know that they were right for Charlie. We may have given each other momentary happiness, but what we had is nothing compared to what Charlie and Elia share now.

Someday, hopefully soon, I'll have that kind of joy in my own life.

ELIA

I'M in the bathroom alone, and I'm glad it's a single stall.

The space is dark, but the room offers just enough lighting. I slip my dress from my shoulders and admire the tan that has started to cover my whole chest. Sunbathing topless was not really something I would have wanted to do, but it was Ainsley who convinced me, pointing out that I really don't want tan lines for the wedding, even if my wedding is four months away.

My breath is coming out hard as I look at myself, and then laugh out loud. Who is this woman looking back at me? She looks happy and healthy with her dark hair pulled back into a high ponytail and a tiara sitting on her head.

I hold up my phone, grabbing one of my breasts and pinching my nipple. I'm so focused on how the rest of the photo looks, that the lighting is right, that my tits are easily visible, that I'm not looking at the camera like I wanted. It suits the image. I'm biting my lower lip in a mix of focus and daring. Knowing that if I try to take another, I'll lose my nerve. I send the text to Charlie with a simple caption.

Look, babe, no tan lines.

Thinking of him getting the text thrills me. I imagine him fisting himself, looking at the picture, and how his hand will slide along his shaft as he thinks of me. Quickly, I pull up my new dress, glad that it zips on the side. My sash slides over my head and I check that my crown is straight. I'm ready to face the rest of the night.

My phone buzzes with a response as I step out of the bathroom and I open it, desperate to see his reply.

> Hmm, I think I'm going to need to inspect it closer. Please send further images for verification.

I snap a selfie with a kissy face before sending it off to him. Still emboldened, I text him again.

> I would much rather you take an up-close-and-personal look at my bare pussy.

His response is almost immediate and I have to flatten the phone to my chest. It's a picture of his cock with his hand wrapped around it, exactly how I imagined.

> Is it bad form to jerk off to thoughts of sinking inside you while I'm at dinner with friends? You've been gone for less than forty-eight hours and I'm already desperate to taste you. You deprived me of morning sex before you left.

I chuckle, thinking of the morning I left. Charlie has been better about not waking up at insane hours anymore, but some mornings he's restless and still wakes at four to work out. Rather than have my alarm wake me, Charlie pressed a kiss to my forehead, stirring me from sleep. It's the only way I want to be woken up ever again.

> More like my tongue sliding along you from base to tip so I can taste you, leaving a rim of my red lipstick on the base of your cock as I suck on you. I want to feel you in my mouth, all of you. Have I ever told you that you make me actually crave blow jobs? I want to feel you explode into my mouth and drink you down.

What a filthy mouth you have indeed. When we're home I'm going to fuck your face, but I won't come in your mouth. I'm going to slide my wet cock along your clit until you're begging me to—

I don't get to finish reading the text.

"You okay, Elia? You look a little flushed," Vivian says with genuine concern.

"You're also breathing weird," Taryn points out, looping her arm in with mine while leading us down the hallway toward a club.

I hate both of them. Only Ainsley is keeping her thoughts to herself and I don't know if that's because she knows the contents of my texts or because she's content to let the other two fuss over me. Maybe they know too and they're just making fun of me.

"Totally fine." My voice could use some work on the convincing front. Ainsley's smirk is all the confirmation for me to know that she knows. "This is the club?" I ask, gesturing at the club we're now standing outside of.

"Uh, yes. Are you sure you're okay?" Vivian asks again.

"Just tipsy and getting soberer by the minute. Let's keep this bitchy bach going!" I actually whoo.

Kill me now.

While Vivian is checking us in, I take a peek at my phone to read the rest of the text only to see that more has come through, including a photo of the tip of Charlie's cock with cum on it.

Fuck me.

This is what you do to me.

This power I hold over him is a potent thing. A man like Charlie demands respect. He pushes through acquisitions. He's a leader while others follow him. It's all I can do to not dry hump my phone while it vibrates. This man makes me desperate to feel him.

Who knew going without sex for two days could be so brutal?

Why is it that my desire is strongest when I can't get my hands on him?

The hostess leads us to a corner booth. For just the four of us, there is more than enough space. I shoot off a text telling Charlie I'm going radio silent and that I love him. I would come up with something more clever, but my best friends are here to celebrate me, and it's rude of me to ignore them while I sext my fiancé.

For the most part, the white dress and crown keep handsy guys at bay. A few get overly friendly, offering a hookup before I have one penis forever. I'm not sure what about the bridal white makes men think that I'm interested in risking that before I get to marry the man of my dreams. They never understand when I say that this one cock is all I need in my life.

At the center of the space are several raised daises with poles for people to get up and grind on them with their friends. It runs the risk of creeps looking up your skirt, but I'm a good girl and keep my knees together whenever Vivian and I indulge. We do shots and bounce between the dance floor and our booth until we're all loose and letting the music guide us. I have the feeling of being watched while on the small stage, but shake it off because of course people are watching us. We're hot chicks dancing on a platform for everyone to see.

Vivian abruptly hugs me to her, startling me. "I feel like I should send Charlie a gift basket!" she shouts to be heard over the music.

I must have heard her wrong. "*What?!*" I shout back, confused.

Vivian is unsteady on her feet, slurring her words a little. "I feel like I should send him a gift basket. If he hadn't hit you with that car or taken care of you, we may never have reconnected. I don't think I'll stop being thankful to him for giving you back to me."

Tears prick my eyes and I hug her close.

"I love you," I tell her, squeezing the life out of her. "We're family. I would have found my way back to you, I'm sure of it."

"I love you too!" she shouts.

"Dance, bitches!" Taryn calls from below us. I see Ainsley across the room dancing with some guy, but she looks happy where she is, her head tossed back as she grinds on the guy's thigh before kissing him.

Vivian and I slip down and I wipe at my eyes. "I'm going to get a drink," I shout and they both nod, holding up their full glasses. I turn and walk toward our booth.

It's a mob scene in the club, and I'm shouldering past people, trying to get back to the table. I've done an excellent job of straddling the line of trashed and buzzed. Usually, water is a commodity in Vegas, but thankfully our table service came with it.

I'm almost back at the table when strong hands grab my hips, pulling me into the seat of a man's pants. As he leans in close to be heard over the music, his hot breath on my neck sends a shiver skittering down my spine.

"Where do you think you're going?"

Nine

TARYN

HANDS GRAB my hips from behind and I spin around, ready with my usual retort, but I come up short.

"Brad?!" I shout.

"In the flesh!" he confirms.

I pull my hand back and hit him on the chest. "What are you doing here?"

"What am I doing here? I came here for you," he tells me like this is all the explanation I need. I hate to admit that he looks good with the top two buttons open on his black button down and his brown hair combed neatly to the side.

"I'm here for your future sister-in-law's bachelorette party. Not to hook up with some guy." When I turn to look at Vivian, she's dancing with an admittedly very good-looking guy who is peppering kisses all along her neck. I don't know what I expected from a club called *Aphrodisiac*. Maybe this was not the best location for a bachelorette party.

"I know you are, but I had to come and see you. I didn't like how we left things."

Tired of shouting, I grab him and drag him back to our booth. I don't see Elia, but she probably went to the bathroom or I passed her on the dance floor. This place is crowded because some popular DJ is playing.

"How we left things?" I ask once we're in the booth. I pour myself a drink and offer one to him, which he gladly takes.

"Yeah, your last text to me was all, 'Don't count on it,' but I thought maybe I should come and make my case. The last time you were in my bed was the last time I was happy."

I think back to the last time we hooked up. All that comes to mind is before I took my internship calling him in a panic about what if the guys I work with don't respect me and how I should best approach that. I'm pretty sure that conversation ended with Brad's dick in my mouth while I got him hard before he fucked me facedown into his mattress.

"The last time I was with you I was telling you I was worried about not being taken seriously in the office and your response was to have sex, like that was the answer. I don't want to keep just having sex, Brad. And if I do, I don't want it to be with you. You don't see me as anything more than a blow-up doll at your beck and call."

He downs his drink angrily. It's not an action I would ever think to assign an emotion to, but somehow he captures it.

"That is not true, Taryn, and you know it. We have a connection. I know we do. I came all the way out here for you."

"You came all the way out here for you. Don't put this on me," I shout back at him.

Brad grabs my face and kisses me, and damn it if I don't want to melt into him. Kissing Brad is familiar, and that's what I yearn for. I know each move he's going to make before he does it. His tongue brushes against my lip, waiting for me to open to him, to deepen the kiss. There is no romantic spark between us, even if I wanted there to be one, which I don't. Charlie and Elia have seriously fucked me for what I want in a relationship. I want that moony-eyed, I-need-you-like-I-need-air feeling. With Brad, it's more like, I-need-you-like-I-need-a-hole-in-my-head.

But there is something to be said about being with someone who already knows that you like getting a finger in the ass every now and then, even if it makes you feel dirty. It's why I keep coming back to Brad, even though there's nothing more than mediocre sex between us.

His hand is on my knee, moving up the side of my thigh. I have to really think about if I want him between my legs. There is none of that flush of arousal, none of that pussy-clenching need, but I'd be lying if I said I couldn't use a pick me up in the form of an orgasm. Maybe one last fuck would do me good. This club has enough dark corners that I could make it work, but—

No buts.

No.

I push him off and then slap him for good measure. Brad was already anticipating the strike because he was pulling his face back, and I wonder how often he's found himself in similar situations. My hand glances off his chin, and he touches it like I've delivered a killing blow.

"What was that for?!" he demands.

I stand up and leave him in the booth without an answer.

If he doesn't get it now, he never will.

Ten

AINSLEY

MAGIC LIPS. The guy I'm kissing has to have magic lips because he's leaving tingly traces of his mouth as he moves down my neck. His fingers moving inside me to the measured thrust of my hips as I grind against his legs help too.

I cast a surreptitious glance around the room to see if anyone is watching us. It would be so easy to straddle this man and ride him like one of the Horsemen of the Apocalypse going into battle. I want to ride him until we are both nothing but weary bones. His cock is pressing against my thigh and from the feel of him, I know I would be satisfied.

Then my eyes catch on something unexpected: Elia. I can't see her face, but her dress glows even in the dark of the room. There is some guy with her and he's pushing her into one of the bathrooms, closing the door behind him.

Quickly, I disentangle myself from the guy I'm with. I don't offer him an explanation. I just push and shove people, ready to claw someone's eyes out. The smart thing probably would have been to drag him with me. I could use some muscle because I'm short, but that just means I'm the perfect height for a junk punch.

I'm not certain which bathroom it was, so I just start pushing on doors regardless of what it says on the outside. For all I know it's like the movie with Liam Neeson and someone is dragging Elia out the back of the kitchens.

The first door is the men's room, and one of the guys has the audacity to shake his limp cock at me, as if I want a piece of it.

"I've had bigger sausages for breakfast. Excuse me if I'm not impressed," I snap.

Only one door doesn't open to me. Something must be blocking it.

"Not today, motherfucker," I mutter under my breath, throwing my shoulder into the door. It takes several attempts of throwing myself into it before it finally opens. There was a fancy ottoman blocking the door that I want to kick, but I need to help my friend.

Elia isn't screaming, but that doesn't mean that she's not in trouble. This guy could have a gag in her mouth or something equally horrible. Neither of them seem to notice me. He's holding her hands over her head and he has her pinned to the wall.

"Get the fuck off her!" I scream. I don't think, I just fly across the room with a kidney punch before I start to slam on his back with my fists. In hindsight, maybe I should have gotten security before coming in here.

"Oww. Fuck. Ainsley, stop!" a familiar voice calls, and I finally look past my true crime-loving red haze of the worst-case scenario and see that it's Charlie shielding Elia's bare chest with his body.

"Charlie?" I ask, surprised. "You're supposed to be in New York." Relief has me dropping my hands to my side.

"I was and then my dumbass brother let himself be led by the cock to Taryn, who I don't think particularly wants to see him, but I wasn't going to pass up the chance to see Elia."

"Hi, Ainsley," she squeaks, looking out from behind his shoulder. She pulls up her dress, and Charlie sets her on the ground.

"I'm going to go and pretend like this never happened. I'll put an out of order sign in front of the bathroom until you're done... you know. So you can... I'm just leaving. Bye!"

"Ainsley!" Charlie calls, stopping me as I reach for the handle. I turn to face him. "Thank you for looking out for Elia."

I don't say anything else as I turn around and leave them. My face is burning with embarrassment, but also I feel intense relief that it was just Charlie with her. Still, I pop up onto the platform to do a spot check of my friends. Vivian and Taryn are chatting in the booth, and I drop down with relief, heading to warn Taryn that Brad might be looking for her.

Eleven

ELIA

CHARLIE'S HEAD drops onto my shoulder with a laugh. Of all the things that I imagined could have happened, getting interrupted by Ainsley was not one of them.

We both chuckle, but when our eyes meet it's like there was no interruption. There is only now. Whatever spark from being away from each other has been kindled into a full blazing inferno. I need to feel him.

Reaching between us, I grab his cock and the man shudders, pressing his hips forward into my hand.

"Where were we?" I ask, a breath before his mouth descends on mine.

Charlie's hands start gripping my face with great care and amazement, before he lets them travel down my body, pulling my dress back down. The cold air is a shock against my bare breasts, but Charlie is quick to cup one while he drags his mouth from mine down my neck.

I moan as he sucks and bites me just above my shoulder. I grip him tighter as desire pools low in my belly. Charlie thrusts forward again, and I move both my hands to his belt so I can free his impressive cock from his pants.

"Oh fuck," he grinds out, slamming his fist against the wall above my head when I tease his cock with the tips of my nails.

I open my eyes to see just how undone my future husband is. With my dress pushed up over my hips, I kiss my way down his chest, wanting to be skin to skin with him. I could insist we go back to one of our hotel rooms, but there is something about the risk of getting caught again that makes my skin burn hotter. It already happened once and could so easily happen again.

"I missed you," I tell him plainly as I sink to my knees.

"Oh, Els," he starts, but all talking is cut short when I wrap my lips around his cock. With one hand I grab his ass, pulling him toward me while the other squeezes his balls. I suck hard on him, letting my teeth graze his shaft until I get to his head, where I swirl my tongue around the tip, letting it trace the slit before I pull off him with an audible pop.

"Pretty sure you promised to fuck my face," I tell him boldly.

Charlie grabs my shoulders, hauling me up before his mouth connects with mine in a searing kiss. My fingers thread through his locks, mussing them as I tug, when he slips one hand between my legs, finding me wet and wanting.

"God, you're so fucking perfect," he whispers before kissing me again.

I pull away, breathless. "All I heard was fucking and I'm wondering why you're not in me yet."

Charlie's pupils are blown as he looks down on me hungrily before lifting me up and pinning me against the wall. I reach between us to grab hold of him and guide him to my entrance. His first stroke into me is slow and careful. Charlie looks down at me with so much love in his eyes that I want to cry. Instead, I grab his face, kissing him hard as he picks up his hip movements.

As he focuses on each punishing thrust, I look away to see our joining in the mirror. For a moment it's like an out-of-body experience to watch him move inside me.

With each thrust, our movements get more and more frenzied.

My hands tighten in his hair, forcing Charlie's head back as I reach the zenith of my orgasm and I shatter around him, my muscles clenching.

I start to cry out, but Charlie clamps his hand over my mouth. Nothing can stop the explosion of pleasure. This seems to egg Charlie on because his head drops forward and he's biting on my collar to stop his own loud groans while he comes.

We're both panting when I finally unlock my legs from around him. Gingerly, he lowers me to the ground. Charlie waits for me to be steady before he releases me. Once the haze of lust clears from his eyes, he's quick about tucking himself away before helping me fix my dress. He brushes a gentle kiss to the spot where he bit me.

"I was a little rough. I'm sorry," he tells me sweetly.

I glance at the two of us. We look like a couple that's been thoroughly fucked, and I'm not sure there is much we can do to fix our appearance. My fingers snag on a few knots in my hair as Charlie tries to flatten his.

"I didn't hate it," I tell him with a smile.

"Minx," he scolds gently.

"We should go. I'm sure the bathroom attendant has waited as long as she could."

"I slipped her five hundred. Ainsley shouldn't have been able to get past her for that amount."

He pushes the ottoman that he had used to block the door out of the way before sliding his hand into mine. My whole body feels raw, as if each touch from him could pull another orgasm from me. I'm sober as a judge and want to spend the rest of the night in his arms, but that wouldn't be fair to my friends who came here to be with me.

"I should get back—" I start, but Charlie interrupts me.

"Dance with me, and then go have fun with your girls. It's made me crazy missing you. When I got home after work on Friday, the sheets smelled like you and all I could think about was what you were wearing and how badly I wanted you in bed with me. You make me insane."

"Don't put your inability to control your dick on me."

The music throbs around us like a pulse as people move seemingly in slow motion in the strobe lights.

Charlie pulls me to his chest before kissing my nose. "No, I'm not. But I also know you love knowing the effect you have on me."

"One dance," I promise him.

But we both know that I'll never be done with him.

Twelve

VIVIAN

VIVIAN

"SO, wait, both Breckenridge brothers are here?" I ask Ainsley, who nods while sipping her drink. She casts her eyes out on the dance floor, finding where Charlie and Elia are dancing like they're the only ones in the room. I should be annoyed, or maybe even mad that the Breckenridge brothers have managed to crash the bachelorette. But at this point, I've realized that *nothing* about this trip is going to go according to plan and only an obscene amount of tequila will make it better.

"Yeah, I actually ran into Brad on the dance floor. He's a big cry baby about Taryn rejecting him so I think I'll give him a pity fuck when he's done sulking. The guy I was hitting it off with had his face glued to another chick so that option is gone."

"I'm sorry, I didn't realize I got us bottle service at a sex club," I whine. Really, I can't begrudge anyone their happiness, and mine is a self-imposed dry spell.

"There is nothing stopping you from sampling the offerings," Ainsley points out.

"You're absolutely right. There is nothing to stop me, but I don't know. Is it so bad that I just want to not worry about men? I jumped right into Jack's bed after breaking things off with Connor. I think I've earned some me time."

"Of course you have, but there's no reason to let your pussy dry out. You deserve to have good sex. You deserve to have fun. If you don't want to, I get it, I'll back off, but I don't think you should let yourself suffer."

I hate that I have to shout this conversation. This is something I would rather talk about casually over mimosas, not screaming across the table. Maybe tomorrow when we're all hungover and I need something less painful to think about. I've always been envious of Ainsley's ability to let go and have one-night stands. I'm too guarded, too careful, too anxious to try.

At the thought of having a hangover, I chug one of the mini water bottles they gave us. The closer I get to thirty, the worse the hangovers get. I want to go back to the days of being able to rally the next day.

Ainsley rises abruptly and pulls me to my feet and out onto the dance floor. Slowly we make our way toward Elia, but halfway there, we find Taryn dancing on her own, which is surprising. There isn't a gaggle of guys around her trying to woo her into their beds, and she must be glad of it after how Brad crashed this weekend for her.

Elia catches my eye, and she drags Charlie over to where we're dancing. It's not as awkward as I thought it would be, but Charlie knows he's crashing, so he gives his bride-to-be a kiss on the cheek and heads in the direction of our table service at her gesturing.

Even though Elia's dancing with us, she's eye-fucking him in the booth. They share a type of love that one can only hope for. It hasn't had to stand the test of time yet, but I know that it will.

"Stop fucking him from the dance floor. If you want to get some, *get it,*" Taryn urges.

"Oh, she already did," Ainsley shouts.

Even in the haze of the lights, I can see how Elia flushes at being outed. "I am here to be with you three, not Charlie. He knows it."

"Did he bring anyone fun with him that I might know?" Ainsley asks.

Elia looks clueless and shrugs. "We, uh, didn't talk much." Her confession has her blushing again while I lean in and cheer for her.

When we go back to the booth to get drinks a while later, Charlie and his friends have taken over. Brad is sitting on one side of him, sullenly drinking from one of our cups while Charlie is engaged in a heated conversation with a Black man. All three of them look at us when we show up. The way Charlie's friend is looking at me makes me think of what Ainsley suggested.

I've never been a casual hookup girl. Serial monogamy is the name of my game, but maybe I should give casual a try. The man's dark eyes linger first on my breasts, then on my long legs, before landing on my eyes.

I don't have to have sex with the man. Maybe a no strings attached make-out would do me some good. Elia steps over the guy, kissing him on the cheek before settling on Charlie's lap, ensuring that there is enough space for all of us. Ainsley crushes three shots before dragging Brad away so Taryn doesn't have to face him.

"I'm Walt!" the man shouts, holding his hand out to me. I shake it, firmly settling next to him while Taryn sits on Charlie's other side.

Taryn eyes Charlie and Elia then me and Walt. I could swear I see her mouth 'déjà fucking vu' before engaging with the happy couple.

"I'm Vivian," I tell Walt. "How do you know Charlie?" The familiarity that Elia showed when greeting him makes me feel insecure for some stupid reason. I didn't think there were very many people in Elia's life that I didn't know, especially ones that she knows well enough to greet with a kiss.

"Charlie and I went to prep school together. I guess it's best to get this all out of the way before the big day."

"All the awkward small talk? What better place for it than at a club?" Clubs are not for small talk, but Walt laughs good-naturedly. His arm stretches along the back of the bench, and I'm surprised when I feel his fingers graze the nape of my neck.

"We could go find somewhere quiet?" he offers, leaning in so he's not shouting at me.

"I'm Elia's maid of honor. I can't ditch her bachelorette for small talk."

"Honey, there is nothing small about me."

I can't help it, I laugh in his face. His smile makes me think he realizes just how ridiculous he sounds.

"I would apologize for laughing but I won't."

Walt leans forward and pours us both drinks. I probably shouldn't have another. We've been drinking for hours now, and I don't see that slowing down.

"You shouldn't have to. I just don't want to have to sit next to Chelia when they decide to fuck in the booth."

"Chelia?"

"Yeah, like their ship name," he clarifies, like I don't know what a ship is.

"Are you a...*nerd*?" I ask, intrigued.

"Dramione but none of that Reylo shit. I will fuck with Finnpoe and Obi-Wan is a ship onto his own."

That's it, I think I will have sex with this man I barely know. Who knew talking nerdy to me was the fastest way to get into my pants? When I reach for my drink, I catch sight of Taryn, and it makes me pause. Charlie is lazily stroking the outside of Elia's thigh while still engaging in a conversation. Taryn is trying to focus on the two of them, but I can confirm that when they cuddle like this, it's hard to talk to them because it makes you feel almost like a voyeur.

"Taryn!" I shout, beckoning her to our side of the bench. Her head snaps toward me, her shoulders slumping in relief. She obliges because it gives her something to do.

"You summoned?" she asks, tucking close into my side.

"Where do you stand on the Reylo argument?" Walt asks her, giving me a wink. Since I drew Taryn over, he's given me physical space while still remaining close enough to us to talk.

We fall down the nerd rabbit hole, discussing everything from Star Wars to Marvel to movie reboots. I hate to admit it, but this is the most relaxed Elia has been outside the massage since we got here. I don't know if it's that we're not going crazy or if it's having Charlie by her side, but I'm not going to begrudge her it at all.

Ainsley and Brad finally return, completing our group. Both their appearances are a little mussed, hair looking like it's been teased and tugged. Perhaps Brad got his pity fuck after all. Taryn glances at them, but turns her attention back to the point she was arguing with Walt.

Elia perks up. "I want to gamble."

"She's going to bankrupt us, isn't she?" Charlie asks no one in particular.

Our group moves on to the casino floor.

Tonight, Charlie is on a mission, leading us through the floor toward the table games and up past the velvet ropes where the high roller section is. Taryn blanches, and I don't blame her. The minimum bet on some of these tables is more than the rent on my first New York City apartment.

Charlie is talking with one of the room attendants. When they mention how much he has to prove he has to get into the room, most of us balk.

"How many zeros is that?" Taryn asks when he returns.

"Don't worry about it. This is for everyone. Just have fun," Charlie tells her, depositing a stack of $1,000 chips into her palm. Taryn looks almost furious to have several months of her student loan payments just dropped into her hand like a spare twenty. As much as I love Charlie, sometimes I think he's out of touch with the actual value of money, something I know Elia's been talking with him about. It's not that he doesn't understand what that amount means. It's more that he's just so free with it when Taryn, or even I, can't be. I'm in better shape than she is as far as student loan payments go. Pawning jewelry from Jack certainly helped reduce the burden.

"Charles," Elia admonishes, grabbing his arm and dragging him off to the side. There is an attendant who looks like he wants to do something to serve us, but since Charlie is the one with the line of credit, he doesn't want to interrupt.

"Jeeves, can I get a glass of Macallan?" Brad orders. "For Taryn, she'll have your best champagne. Actually, all the girls will."

Taryn looks torn between throwing the chips in her hand at Charlie or Brad.

"I'll have a vodka, straight," Taryn corrects with a glare.

"Can we actually get ginger ale and saltines?" Charlie says when he turns back to us. His arm is wrapped around Elia, and he's gently rubbing her back.

Everyone starts to put in their orders, and the attendant nods before handing us off to a pretty woman with her hair pulled back into a high ponytail.

"Mr. Breckenridge, if your party will follow me, we'll get you set up."

Charlie, Brad and Walt lead the way while the four of us hang back, linking up our arms.

"We can ditch them," Ainsley suggests.

Elia, who is looking a little green around the gills, shakes her head. "When else are we going to get into a high roller room? No, let's have fun with this. I hate to be a bitch, but I have three single gorgeous friends and we're in a room with whales. Shoot your shot."

"You okay?" I ask, rubbing her back, but she rolls her shoulder, pushing me off. I'm too drunk to control the hurt look on my face, but she shakes her head.

"No, you're fine, but if you rub my back, I will vomit. I cannot hang. I'm trying, I'm trying so hard, but I was actually falling asleep at the club. It just looked like Charlie and I were getting frisky."

"We can go back to the room," I suggest.

"No. We're here to have fun. This isn't just about me and it's only tonight. We fly home tomorrow. I can put on my big girl panties and get through one night."

We try our hand at several different games. Brad keeps trying to weasel closer to Taryn, who still isn't having any of it. He tries by teaching her Blackjack or Let it Ride or any other game where he can move closer to her.

Elia nearly weeps when they bring her some buttered toast, and for the most part it helps her rally. Now that we're free of the noisy club, I'm able to chat more easily with Walt, who I learn is officiating the wedding. That news seals it for me: I cannot sleep with this man, as glorious as he is.

Still, Esme's words about finding love, as unbelievable as they are, linger in the back of my mind. It's not like I have to get engaged. I don't want to be alone. I love love. I loved being wrapped up in another person who knew me so well, who tolerated my quirks and protected me. I'm going to have to get back on the horse again someday. Maybe it's time to stop guarding my heart so viciously.

For tonight, I'll have to settle for some light flirting. Eventually, I'll build back up to wanting to see someone, but tonight is not that night.

Thirteen

TARYN

DISCRETION IS key in places like the high roller room. It's why I feel like I can ask the woman delivering drinks if there is a private place I can go to yell at Brad for not listening when I told him not to come here.

I grab Brad and follow the woman to a side room that she unlocks with a key before she ushers us inside. There is a recliner and a table with some snacks and an eye mask on it. Maybe for high rollers who aren't quite done but need a breather or to get some actual sleep.

Sometimes in a casino you forget how time passes you by and with the bright lights and the extra oxygen they pump in, it's no wonder. I would forget myself for sure.

Brad takes this private room the wrong way, and he moves in to kiss me, but I push him away. Using his size against me, he walks me backward until my back hits the wall. It makes me simultaneously want to scream at him and spread my legs wider. When it was good between us, it was amazing. My breath comes in rough pants, remembering what he's done to me in the past, and how he's done it. I press my mouth to his.

"This is the last time," I tell him as I pull on his pants. His hand grips my braid and tugs my head back just a little to show he has the power. He doesn't, but I let him keep thinking it, because in the end I know that he is the one that got on a plane to fly to me because he missed me. I hold the power over him, even if it is just the power of my pussy.

"You said that last time," he reminds me before kissing me hard.

We're silent as we get dressed, both tense in spite of the release we achieved. Once I find my underwear, I slip them back on, watching him as he straightens himself out. Brad smooths his hand over his hair, using some of the gel in the room. I take advantage of a different mirror, pulling my hair from the braid and quickly redoing it. I can't imagine what our friends are going to think when we walk out there.

Brad finally approaches me, twisting a strand of my hair around his finger and then tucking it behind my ear. "Are you still going through recruiting this fall?"

The question comes so far out of the blue that I stumble. "What?"

"Recruiting...for jobs? Or did you get an offer from the firm where you had your internship?"

My cheeks heat at the thought, and I shake my head. "No, well, yes, but I'm not taking it."

"Why, already got a better offer?"

"No, I'm not a fan of taking hush money."

Looking away from Brad, I move to the door, but he sidesteps to block me. "Hush money?"

"It's a long story, one I don't want to discuss during my

friend's bachelorette. If you want the story, if you want to really be my friend, you can call me when we're back in New York."

Brad looks down, then nods his ascent and opens the door for me.

Turns out, I didn't have to be worried about my friends because they're all circled around the roulette table. Elia is at the center of the excitement.

"What did I miss?" I ask Vivian, stepping behind her.

"Babe, the statistical probability of hitting red for a third time is unbelievable," Charlie tells Elia adamantly. "You should bet on another color."

Elia glares. "What happened to, 'we have money' and 'don't worry about it?'" She's waving her hands like it's all just one big conspiracy.

"You shouldn't worry about it, and we do have money, but your current bet is up to twenty thousand dollars. I worry about how you might take that loss and how you might become a gambling addict forever chasing the high of that time you got red twice in a row."

This almost makes Elia more indignant to prove him wrong. The dealer glances between the two of them before announcing, "No more bets."

Elia claps, and Charlie wraps his arms around her chest, holding her close to him. When the ball lands on red for the third time, she nearly breaks his nose jumping up and down.

Walt, who is nursing his drink across the table, shakes his head, aghast. "Walk away, Elia."

Elia looks at the growing stack of chips beside her original bet.

"You've created a monster," I tell Charlie, who nearly jumps at my sudden arrival. If he notices how disheveled I look, he doesn't comment.

"I have. Looks like I'm going to have to keep her out of the casinos."

"Place your bets," the dealer calls. With Elia's success, we've garnered a crowd. Even Ainsley has rejoined the group. When she catches my eye, she smirks then taps her lips. I run my hand under my mouth, annoyed that my finger comes away with my lipstick. The lighting in the private room was too dark for me to fully notice the smudges. Though I've avoided looking at him until now, one glance at Brad shows that he has my lipstick smeared on his mouth too.

Color-stay my ass.

A man steps forward, challenge on his face. "I'm willing to match your bet that it won't happen again. Actually, I'll double that bet." The man is short and thin, and, honestly, obnoxious as he counts out eighty thousand dollars. My stomach turns at the sight of it. Elia ignores him.

Charlie runs a hand through his hair, oblivious to the conversation happening between Ainsley and me. The dealer clears the bet, and I realize that Elia is staying on red. With a quick count of her chips, she's betting forty thousand dollars like it's nothing. She's betting it like she's got millions at home, which she does, but that doesn't mean watching her bet an amount like that doesn't hurt.

Our group holds its breath watching the ball spin around the wheel and ticking against each pocket as it slows until it catches on a black hole before rolling to a stop in red.

Everyone erupts with cheering, including the strangers watching. I don't think Elia has a full grasp on what just happened, because she's just staring at the dealer as he counts out the chips until Charlie lifts her and spins her. The only man not celebrating is the one who just lost. Trying to capture Elia's good luck, he drops an equally large stack on red.

"Place your bets," the dealer calls, and Elia pushes on Charlie to grab her chips.

"I'm out," she tells everyone hurriedly. Charlie helps her pull her chips out of play. Grabbing a handful of chips, she gives them to the dealer as a tip before Charlie hugs her close to him. I'm not privy to what he whispers to her, I want to give them a moment, so I watch the next round begin.

Elia is shaking her head at whatever Charlie said. An observant attendant, the same woman who directed Brad and me to a room, steps forward to collect Elia's winnings. The woman is turning with the chips on a tray when the ball stops.

Black.

Charlie is quick to pull Elia into his side, while Brad and Walt step in the way, seemingly to follow the couple, but mostly to show the man with murder in his eyes that Elia is off limits. It's his own fault for betting like that. When I do the math, I feel disgusted. He bet more than my annual salary in a five-minute span and lost.

I guess they're right; the casino does always win.

"You realize you just tipped that man twenty grand, right?" Brad asks.

Elia turns white, then glances over her shoulder as if she can somehow claw back the tip. Charlie presses a kiss to the top of her head.

"Someone should tell you, love, we're rich," he teases her with a laugh.

We circle and play a few different games, including Blackjack at Vivian's behest, and it's the only game that Elia will play again. She's gunshy after her big winnings, keeping her bets low. It's selfish and not in the spirit of things, but I hold on to the money Charlie gave me to bet with.

"Spend it," Ainsley orders out of the corner of her mouth as Vivian is arguing with Charlie and Walt over whether she should split her sevens.

"What?" I ask, spinning the chips in front of me. Our group is so large we have essentially taken over a table for just us.

"Spend it," she repeats, turning to face me.

"I'm just waiting for the right moment," I lie.

"No, you're not. You're going to hoard those chips and cash them into your account at the end of this. Just place a bet."

"I can't," I whisper, shaking my head. "The massages were stretching me a touch further than I could afford, but I wanted to do something for Elia. I felt like a freeloader. The minimum bet at this table is more than my monthly loan payment."

Ainsley smirks, then sips from her drink. Seeing something on my face, probably my reaction to the smirk, she coughs. "I'm not laughing at your plight, but you also don't have to worry about the massages."

"What?"

"I wasn't going to tell you, but I had them switch the charge card when we went." Ainsley seems unbothered by her confession.

"Why would you do that?" I demand, heat rising in my cheeks.

"Why wouldn't I do that? What am I supposed to do? Listen to my friend tell me about her struggles and then ignore a small way to help her when I can?"

"You're supposed to mind your own fucking business, Ainsley."

Ainsley rears back, then laughs. I can hear how forced it is, and we've caught the attention of everyone else.

"Everything okay?" Brad asks, putting his hand on my back, but I shove him off.

"I'm perfectly capable of taking care of myself. If I wanted help, I would ask for it. The rest of you flaunt your money well enough for me to know you could bail me out if I wanted you to. I don't need your help, and I don't want it."

"Yes, you do," Ainsley says. "You're just too stubborn to ask."

"Go fuck yourself, Ainsley. You have no right to tell me how to live my life, not when you'll fuck anything that shows an interest in you."

Ainsley goes red, but takes a deep breath. "I'm not going to let you bait me. If you think you need to slut shame me to make yourself feel better, then fine. It doesn't stop me from being right."

"Maybe we should take this back a notch?" Elia asks, grabbing my hand and physically pulling me back.

"Maybe you should stay out of this. You're just as bad as them, betting forty thousand dollars."

"Enough," Charlie growls, naturally stepping in to protect Elia. She too has turned red and is looking away from me.

"Why don't we call it a night?" Vivian suggests.

I want to lash out at her, but seeing the looks on everyone's faces, my anger fades.

Brad reaches for me again, but I flinch out of his grip with a shake of my head. "Stop," I order.

Brad holds his hands up defensively, then turns to cash out to end the game they were all in the middle of before I ruined things with my pride. Some small, sober part of me might appreciate what Ainsley has done, but I wish she had just talked to me about it instead of assuming she knew better.

Am I stretched thin? Yes. But does that mean she needs to come in and cover my rent whenever that happens? No.

There is stilted silence among the group as we walk out. Vivian hangs back with me, sliding her hand into mine.

"I'm sorry," I say, desperate to get the words out as regret weighs on me.

"I'm not the one you need to apologize to."

When we reach the exit to the casino, Charlie stops short. "Chad?" he asks.

We move around him to see who he's talking to. Sitting on the ground, leaning against a support pillar, is one of his fraternity brothers that I recognize from college.

"Yep." Chad's tone is clipped. He lifts his head to squint at us. When looking up becomes too difficult, he lets his head loll to the side.

"Where have you been? I lost sight of you at the club," Charlie says, kicking Chad's foot gently, unsure if he has fallen asleep.

There is silence as we wait, and Charlie kicks his foot again.

Chad lifts his head suddenly. "Got kicked out."

"For what?" Walt asks.

"Booted. On the floor. And some chick. And I think a security guard." Chad's eyes close and he lets his head drop forward.

"Let's get you back to the hotel. Seems like tonight was a big night for you," Charlie says with a laugh as Walt and Brad help Chad up.

"I'll get Chad back to his room," Ainsley offers.

Chad vigorously shakes his head. "I'm not done yet. Gotta go to the Bellagio."

"What, so you can boot there?" Walt asks with a chuckle.

"Boot?" Elia asks. Her face says she knows what we're hinting at, but she wants to make sure.

"Vomit," I clarify.

The look on Elia's face says she wants to do just that at the thought.

"That's why we say boot," Charlie explains, tugging his fiancé closer to him.

"I'm not sure a cab driver will let him in a vehicle," Vivian points out, looking green around the edges as she points at his shirt. That's when I notice that he has some sick on his shirt.

Elia looks like she's going to lose it at any moment and has to walk away.

"I'll take care of Chad. Get your girl home," Walt tells Charlie.

Chad shoulders everyone off. "I'm fine. I'm feeling lucky." Once free of everyone, Chad sways a little but pulls his shirt off.

"Go buy him a shirt," Charlie tells his brother, handing him a few bills and pointing him in the direction of the hotel.

Brad reluctantly glances at Chad then me before listening to the instructions and setting off to find Chad a shirt. I'm not minding the view as Chad lazily scratches at his six pack. He is all sorts of eye candy and always has been.

"Seriously, get Elia back to the room," Vivian tells Charlie.

One glance at the bride-to-be, and I see she's swaying on her feet for a totally different reason. Her blinks are getting longer and at some point she must have rubbed her eyes because her mascara has created a dramatic raccoon eye.

"We've got Chad," I assure him.

"And I already added you lot to brunch tomorrow," Vivian tells him.

Charlie looks between Chad and Elia before he nods. "Will the rest of you be okay getting back?"

"No! We should stay with everyone," Elia insists with another slow blink.

Charlie scoops her up in one swift movement, hugging her frame to his chest. "Enough. To bed with you," he orders as a black car pulls up in front of us.

"To sleep or to fuck?" she asks dreamily, nuzzling her face into his neck.

Charlie chuckles. "Let's see how conscious you are when we get to the room and we can make a decision then. How about that?"

Vivian's thumbs fly over her screen as she hurriedly texts Charlie, I'm sure with information about brunch in the morning. Though I would be surprised to see them before our flight tomorrow.

As much as this weekend was for Elia, it was good to get away from Manhattan, even if it was only for a couple of days. Brad returns shortly, confused about where his brother has gone, but seeing that Elia is also missing, it's not hard for him to piece together what happened.

"So, assuming they're likely going to go fuck, what do you boys say to coming back to our room and playing Kings?" Ainsley offers.

Chad manages to pull on his 'I Love Sin City' shirt. With a grin, he nods. "Let's keep the party rolling."

Fourteen

AINSLEY

I WAKE up with the sun, and I'm mad about it. I'm sleeping on the couch with my head in Chad's crotch, and I'm pretty sure I can feel his morning wood pressing against my forehead. Our mistake last night after coming back to the room was leaving the blinds open so we could gaze down on the neon lights of Vegas.

There must be hundreds of rooms like ours that are now suffering as the sun crests the mountains. My shoulder is stiff, and when I roll over, I'm surprised to find Chad is awake.

"Ains," he whispers in greeting, "you drool."

"And your cock is poking me in the face," I point out, sitting up.

"What can I say? There is something about having a hot chick's face near Hotrod that makes him real hard."

I scoff. "Hotrod?"

"Does your pussy not have a name? I bet if I get acquainted, I could come up with a good name for her."

And that's how I wind up fucking Chad in the bathroom, biting his shoulder as I come while I straddle him on the bench in the shower.

Chad is decidedly less quiet with his release, not caring if he wakes the rest of our friends, who are sprawled about the room. When we left everyone they were all still asleep. Vivian and Walt are snuggling on the bed, fully clothed, while Brad is folded in a chair and Taryn has a bed all to herself.

Well-acquainted with each other's bodies, Chad and I shower together. I lean into calling his dick 'Hotrod' before I suck on him, even going as far as begging for it as he eats me out.

When we emerge, everyone else is still asleep, so I leave a note letting them know that the shower is open and that I'll see them all at brunch.

A few hours and orgasms later, Chad and I are approaching the restaurant. Only after we were leaving the room did Chad admit to having his own room. I didn't mind because it meant having some highly energetic loud sex in his own room, but it also means we're the last to arrive at brunch. The brunch spot Vivian found is a cheery fifties-style restaurant with diner food. The idea of guzzling greasy diner food is what keeps me moving at this point.

"Where is the bride?" I ask, sliding into the booth.

A hand shoots up from the booth beside Charlie. "She's here," Charlie confirms, his hand staying under the table.

"Then good god, man, let her up. Blow jobs at the brunch table are indecent. I know it's Vegas baby, but there are still some lines you do not cross. And I thought catching you two fucking in the club was bad," I tease.

Elia's head pops up and she practically growls from behind her thick, dark sunglasses.

"Come off it, Ainsley. It's not like you haven't fucked someone in public," Taryn points out. I think she's trying to keep the accusation in her tone light, but she's still pissed at me. I can't blame her. I should have talked to her about switching our cards before I did it, but I'm not sorry about helping her.

"Thrice this weekend alone," I say with a laugh.

Brad, sitting next to his brother, turns red.

"Who knew Brad was such a delicate flower?" Taryn says, trying to tease him.

"Especially since he was one of those guys in that same club. I took a page out of Charlie and Elia's book. That bathroom was made for fucking." I'm laughing at how embarrassed Brad is getting, and honestly, he kind of deserves it. Charlie looks a little green at the talk of me and his brother having sex.

When the waitress comes over, I make sure that we have a round of mimosas. Elia groans, leaning into Charlie's side, but doesn't object past that.

"Can we backtrack, for just, like, thirteen seconds? Did you say you slept with Brad last night?" The edge is back in Taryn's voice, and I'm wondering what I did wrong. I know that he said he came there for her and that they had been fooling around, but I know she also said she was done with him.

"Do we really need to discuss this now?" Brad asks. "Did you say you caught Charlie and Elia having sex in a bathroom?"

"No, we really do," Taryn snaps, turning her laser focus back to me.

"Yes, at the club," I say. Then I remember the lipstick smeared on Taryn's face and turn to face Brad, who knows he's caught. "Before we went to the casino."

"What are we missing?" Vivian asks, but then it occurs to her, and she pinches her lips together.

"Ah, so you too explored the Cave of Wonders," Chad says with a knowing nod.

This seems to zap any and all growing animosity in the group.

"I'm sorry, what?" Brad asks, genuinely mystified.

Even I'm confused.

"You've gotten to explore the depths and wonders of—"

All at once, it hits me what he's referring to. "Please, stop," I demand, flustered.

Elia pulls down her sunglasses and gives me a knowing look with a smirk.

"Okay..." Walt looks around. "Besides all the sex, did anyone else win big last night?"

"I actually won a grand on the slots this morning," Taryn confesses with a big smile.

"Looks like everyone has had a little bit of luck this trip," Elia says, perking up as she alternates between water and a mimosa.

"Some more than others," Vivian teases.

"Some less than others," Charlie says pointedly, shooting Brad a look.

"Well, I want to thank everyone for helping make this weekend so much fun. You never failed to keep the mood upbeat, even when things got dire. To new friends and old friends," Elia says, lifting her glass.

We all raise our glasses and clink them together.

When Elia slips out of the booth after our food is delivered, I follow her, even though I feel kind of weird about it. At the bathroom, she looks surprised to see me on her heels.

"I just wanted to apologize," I tell her, squeezing her forearm gently.

Her surprise turns to confusion as she pushes into the brightly lit room.

"What for?" she asks as we wait for a stall to open up.

"For the club last night." I cast a surreptitious look at the women in front of us.

"No, no, spell it out. You had no problem announcing to our friends what you're apologizing for." She doesn't look mad, only amused, with a wry twist to her lips.

"I'm sorry for attacking Charlie while he was trying to fuck your brains out."

"Better. I thought we were done tiptoeing around the issue."

"I'm not tiptoeing around the issue. I'm just trying to not

announce your business to the whole bathroom." This feels suspiciously like banter.

"Unlike at the brunch table?"

"Yes, well, I guess I should apologize for that too. After what happened at New Years, I feel like I need to aggressively remind people that Charlie and I aren't a thing. So I'm sorry for airing your sex life to anyone who will listen."

"Thank you. I understand that. I'll admit to sometimes being clingier than I would be with Charlie, if only to remind people that I am the one with him and not you. So often we'll go out with his old buddies for the purpose of me meeting them, and someone will inevitably ask about you. I don't have a problem with you. I have a problem with people pretending like I don't matter."

"You know Charlie will cut those people out faster than you can say 'yeet,' right?"

"I know, but I don't want him to do that. Not for me. We've been seeing more of his mother, and I know that makes him happy, but he hasn't spoken to his father since he cleaned out his desk. Charlie doesn't like to talk about it, but I know it was hard on him."

"That's because his father was hard on him, but his father was just one person in his life. You are *the* person in his life. You're his reason for getting up in the morning, and as someone who thought she was that for Charlie, it's actually really sad but amazing to see how different he is with you. I thought I had his whole heart, but I've come to see that I didn't." I want that for myself, that kind of love and devotion. "And since I'm being ladies-room honest with you right now," I continue, "I never gave him my whole heart. After years of being off and on, it was hard to take that leap. I don't regret it, because it brought you into Charlie's life. And knowing what I do about your life before the accident, I find it hard to feel bad that you got hit by a car."

"That is brutal," the woman waiting in front of Elia says,

turning to look at us, aghast that I would actually tell her that I'm glad she got hit by a car.

"No!" Elia exclaims.

"Honestly, it worked out so well because now she's engaged to my ex-fiancé, and I get to fuck whoever I want, so really, we're both living our best lives," I tell the woman with a wink.

"You're something else, Ainsley Seaborn," Elia says.

"Don't you forget it."

Fifteen

VIVIAN

THE WEEKEND, fun as it has been, is coming to a close and I'm actually mad at myself for how glad I am. We've courted disaster a few times, but we are finally back in our room packing.

I'm so optimistic that I let out a relieved breath. Taryn didn't kill Ainsley. Ainsley didn't kill Brad, though the daggers she kept shooting him during brunch for sleeping with both her and Taryn looked like they could have done some damage. And Elia had a good time, even if the highlight was Charlie showing up.

I feel accomplished and positive I never want to do this again.

Being a maid of honor is exhausting. I would much rather get to be one of the bridesmaids who gets told when to show up and how much to pay. Planning these things is like a whole extra job, which I guess is how other people are able to make a career out of professional bridesmaiding and party planning.

Elia comes up and hugs me from behind as I pull the zipper on my bag.

"I can't thank you enough for this weekend," she says, releasing me. My friend drops onto the bed beside the suitcase with a dreamy smile.

"Even if you were traumatized by a stripper?"

"I wasn't traumatized," she objects, but the flush on her cheeks confirms she was, in fact, traumatized.

"I didn't think about that being a problem, and I'm sorry."

Elia waves a hand flippantly. "Please, it will make for a good story in ten years, when I'm less actively traumatized, though I might never look at a waiter the same way again."

"I don't think I can blame you, though for me, I'll be forever wondering if they're that sexy under their clothes."

"Vivian Louise, objectifying people is wrong," she scolds jokingly.

"And I know it."

"Looked like Walt was objectifying you a little at breakfast this morning..." She's waiting for me to spill the tea.

"There may have been some kissing last night," I admit with a sheepish smile. There was a little more than kissing. There were hands and fingers and my first orgasm that wasn't battery-operated. More than that, though, it was nice to talk to someone and feel heard.

What I'm not telling her is how good it felt to be desired. Ending things with Jack was so sudden, and the reasons were good ones. Reconnecting my best friend with her abusive ex because he was jealous of us was a shit thing to do and I'm never sorry I ended things, but there are moments where I catch myself missing him. I've been moving forward, I've been putting him in my rearview, but through throwing myself into work, not through any great effort to heal my heart.

I'm not saying Walt is the guy to heal my heart, but he did a pretty great job of reminding me with his mouth and his hands that there is more to life than work and planning this wedding.

"Some kissing?"

"A lady never tells."

Elia whips her head, glancing around the room.

"What?" I ask.

"No, sorry. Just looking around for this lady you speak of."

"Bitch."

She grins. "Your *favorite* bitch." Elia holds out her pinky to me, and I slide mine into hers.

"Always."

"What do you mean our flight is canceled?" I demand, trying to keep my cool. We have one last step to this trip, and now, *now* everything falls apart?

"Ma'am, I'm sorry, but the flight has been canceled. The inbound flight cannot get out of its location due to a hurricane, and we do not have a plane to put you on." The gate agent is trying to keep her cool with me, but the line of angry customers behind me is only growing as they get a similar notification that the flight has been canceled.

I just happened to be watching the board when it changed from delayed to outright canceled. All the hard-won chill I managed to collect during the weekend is gone with the flippant non-answers I'm getting.

I move my hands off the counter so I can clench them into fists without the flight attendant thinking that I'm going to deck her over this delay. The truth is, I'm trying to stop this tight feeling in my chest from getting out of control. Even when I don't *have* control, I am *in* control of myself. This is my mantra, and I take a calming breath to avoid chewing this woman out. Reacting strongly to my anxiety over *another* unexpected change is not going to get me anywhere.

"Our flight was supposed to depart in less than an hour. If the plane was coming from a region where they're experiencing a hurricane and the origin flight was canceled, your airline knew about it and is being grossly negligent when it comes to the needs of your customers."

The woman's mouth sets in a line. "Was there a question in there?"

"What are our options to get back to New York City? You know, our original destination." Really, I'm the first person talking to her about this; her patience should still be intact. I take a deep breath in through my nose and remind myself that she is the messenger, not the responsible party.

"Best I can do is get you out on a flight tomorrow afternoon," she tells me. "Or I can connect you through Toronto."

A pair of hands are on my shoulders, pulling me back before I can reach across the counter and strangle this woman.

"Thank you for your help. We understand that this is not your fault. I'll let you know what we want to do," Charlie says smoothly.

I let him guide me away from her. It takes a few reminders that I'm an adult and sticking my tongue out at her will not earn me any adult points.

"Down, Killer," Charlie says with a light laugh. When I narrow my eyes at him, he stops.

"What's the word?" Ainsley asks, holding a drink. I can smell the vodka in it from here.

"No plane. Best they can do is connect us through Toronto or we can fly direct tomorrow."

"Another day to gamble? I'm in," Chad says easily. He slips an arm over Ainsley's shoulders and she shrugs.

"I'll just need to email Eloise to move my meetings around, but I'm in for another night," Ainsley agrees. I follow her line of sight as she looks over Chad like he's the special for the night.

"No," Charlie objects immediately. "Chad, you will die from alcohol poisoning if you try to keep going tonight. I certainly will if I try to keep up with you all again. No, give me twenty minutes. And someone keep an eye on Vivian. I get the feeling if she talks to that gate agent again, only one of them will leave this building alive."

Charlie pulls out his phone and strolls away, looking for a quiet spot among the angry travelers and slot machines.

"I just have school tomorrow, so if I miss a class, who gives a fuck," Taryn says diplomatically.

Brad looks to Taryn, then away. "Same for me. I actually don't have anything on Mondays so I'm free if we have to stay another night."

"I love you all, and this has been fun, but no." Elia shakes her head vehemently. "I have kittens that need snuggling."

We're waiting longer than the twenty minutes Charlie promised. All of us are watching him as he paces with his phone pressed to his ear. He rubs the back of his neck before hanging up and walking toward us.

"Did anyone check a bag?" he asks when he finally reaches us. He lingers on the fringe of the group, looking at everyone before turning his focus on Elia.

"Nope, we carried on," Elia confirms.

Brad, Walt and Chad confirm the same.

"Good. Grab your shit. I got us a flight."

Charlie doesn't elaborate, but like good little chickens, we follow him back out through security and to a waiting limo.

"What did you do, Chuck?" Ainsley asks, obediently climbing in as the driver loads all of our bags into the trunk.

"If we're driving back to New York in that, hard pass. I've been around Chad's toxic farts enough for one weekend." Brad's tone is dripping with annoyance.

"We're not driving. Just get in the car, Brad," Charlie orders dryly.

The rest of us climb in, and I'm a little excited to have Walt by my side, even if I still don't know where we're going.

"So, what's the secret?" Taryn asks, popping open the complimentary bottle of champagne. There's hardly enough for each of us to get a sip, but we do, even if I don't think I ever want to see alcohol again.

"Let it be a surprise," Charlie says cryptically. His hand rests on Elia's knee as his thumb rubs circles around her thigh.

I miss that. I miss having someone who is attentive to my every need, anticipating them before there's a problem. Burdens used to be shared and not mine to manage alone. When I felt out of control, I had someone there to help level out my concerns. It made me feel less like it was just me versus the world. I miss having someone to talk to at night and share my thoughts and dreams and worries with.

Walt isn't the answer, but maybe he can be that first step to opening my heart again.

"Vivian?" Walt whispers, drawing me from thoughts of him.

"Mmhmm?" I ask, meeting his dark eyes. They wrinkle around the corners with his laughter.

"I was just wondering if I could call you when we get back to New York." Any question is gone now; it's a statement. This is what he wants.

"I'm going to be honest with you: I'm not really ready for a relationship right now. I've been engaged twice back-to-back, and my last engagement ended in February. God, even saying that out loud is embarrassing."

"Why is it embarrassing?" His thumb absently rubs my shoulder, and while watching that same move between Charlie and Elia filled me with yearning, this only fills me with the desire to get away.

"Because I've been engaged twice. I'm not a woman who takes that lightly. It's also why I don't think getting involved with the man who is officiating my best friend's wedding is the best idea."

"I can respect that. After the wedding, can I call you?"

Charlie robs me of my chance to answer by announcing that we've arrived at our destination. As the last ones into the limo, Charlie and Elia are the first ones out.

"*Finally.*" Elia practically screams once she's outside.

Once we're all out, I notice Charlie is grinning from ear to ear.

I look around, confused, until I realize we're in a plane hangar and there is a plane sitting there with the stairs lowered. It takes me an embarrassingly long amount of time to realize that this is actually a private jet.

"This has to be a joke," Taryn scoffs.

"No. I don't often throw my money around, but when I do, it's to fulfill a promise to my fiancé." It's clear from how they're looking at each other that Charlie and Elia only have eyes for the other.

Sixteen

ELIA

CHARLIE GOT a private jet to fly us to New York, and it is taking a serious amount of control to not jump him on the tarmac. The way Charlie is looking at me tells me he knows *exactly* what I'm thinking.

I didn't need Vegas to tell me I was lucky. I already knew it.

"If you don't marry that man, I will," Vivian whispers in my ear as she skips past me to get onto the jet.

"All this was for me?" I ask Charlie, sliding my fingers in between his as our friends grab their bags and get situated. The way our hands and bodies fit together is a marvel I will never not be in awe of.

"I promised you a private jet, didn't I? What better way to do it than with our friends?"

"I would argue that doing it alone could lead to more naked time," I hedge.

"Miss Daniels, are you insinuating that you would have sex with me on a plane?"

"I would have you on a bed. I would have you on my head. I would have you against a wall. I would have you all night long. I would do you here and there. I would do you anywhere."

"Dirty, filthy, woman. I have just the punishment for you." His wicked grin makes me want to rub my legs together to relieve some of the pressure building.

I would have him anywhere.

It isn't until later, when we're in the air and our friends are either asleep or engrossed in what they're doing, that Charlie pulls me from my chair. There is a mischievous glint in his eyes, and I know I will follow him anywhere.

The flight attendant pointedly does not look up or acknowledge us as she plays a game on her phone, knowing exactly what we're up to as we slip into the small bathroom. It's larger than I expected, but I don't get a chance to take that thought much further because Charlie grabs my hips and sets me on the very small counter.

I let out a surprised squeak, but his mouth is on mine, suffocating the sound. Under me, the sink has turned on, but there is no time for me to really register that as Charlie brings my hand to his throbbing cock.

"I've been thinking about you all morning," he whispers, kissing my neck and back to my mouth.

"You've been with me all morning."

Charlie thrusts into my hand, and I barely stop the moan as I slide my hand down the length of him. Why did I choose leggings, as if I was getting on a six hour long flight with strangers? Why am I not in a skirt or the dress I wore to the club?

"Yes, and for a period of time, you had your head on my lap and I could practically feel your breath on my cock. I had to think of exploding kittens just to stop my hard-on from poking you in the eye."

I chuckle, burying my face in his neck to give him the kisses that I know tease him.

"Are you still thinking about exploding kittens?" I ask, tugging on his earlobe with my teeth.

"No, I'm thinking about making you scream in this tiny room, and hoping that the jet engine is loud enough to muffle the sound."

"Then what are you waiting for? An invitation?"

Charlie savagely grabs the band of my leggings and pulls them down while I push up on my arms so he can do so. He doesn't take my underwear with him, and I appreciate that because the counter is cold. When he places his mouth close to my pussy as he slips my leggings off my feet, I can't think of anything but his hot breath.

"I love you," I tell him as he comes up to my mouth.

"Oh, I know," he says, pulling my underwear to the side. I watch him as he guides himself closer to me before he meets my eye. "I love you too, Elia Daniels, until my dying breath."

And then he's inside me. It's close quarters and awkward with each small jerky movement, but just knowing where we are, that we can be caught at any moment, kicks up my desire. I look down between us, watching him slide in and out of me.

"Fuck," I whimper, digging my heels into his ass. "Touch me."

His pupils are so large and dark, I can barely see the irises as he reaches between us and presses his fingers to my clit.

"If you don't make a sound, I promise to make you scream later," he says, like we aren't going to go home and fuck our brains out.

It doesn't matter, because I am running and jumping over the precipice and falling into my orgasm. My hands on the back of Charlie's neck dig in, and I can't do it, I can't stop the deep moan that claws free.

Charlie covers my mouth with his but it's useless as his release tears through him, bringing his own audible pleasure. As his hip thrusts subside, he pulls out of me before kissing me deeply again and pulling me flush against his body.

With Charlie, there is no other option, no other way than to be all in with him. He peppers soft kisses on my face before helping me back into my leggings.

When he leaves me to clean up so we can at least pretend like we weren't screwing in the bathroom, I marvel over the goodness that is Charlie. I can pretend like it is luck that I get to be with him, but I think it's so much more. It's pure fate that I can call Charlie mine.

Seventeen

AINSLEY

I CLOSE my eyes when Charlie and Elia slip back to the bathroom hand in hand. When Charlie returns alone, looking rumpled and flushed, I want to make a joke with him, the way I might have when in law school or in college, but I don't.

As much as it pains me to admit, my relationship with Charlie isn't what it was even when we were both seeing other people. The tether between us is broken. There is still love and there is still friendship, but that easy familiarity between us is gone. I miss our friendship more than the partnership.

I miss having that one person know me so well that when I get my period, they're ready with a heating pad and my favorite ice cream. To an extent, I miss that close friendship with Charlie, but more than that, I miss having that type of person in my life. Seeing Charlie and Elia gives me hope that I'll be able to find that for myself.

I've used dating apps before. I've tried swiping on someone to see if they could be a good time, but maybe I need to double down. Maybe I need to give it a real try, to try and grow past a quick fuck, and actually go for a relationship. I don't need to be monogamous quite yet, but it doesn't hurt to start looking.

I go into the Sleepless Nights app preferences and change it from casual to semi-serious, letting anyone who sees my profile know that I could want more. Of all the serious dating websites available, this one might be more hookup friendly than others. I know there are some success stories with it, coworkers or friends who found their significant others. This should at least open up the possibility of me finding love again.

This jet is clearly meant for business because we're seated in a little quad with a table between Chad, Brad and me. I'm almost positive Vivian is similarly getting action in the back of the plane, while Taryn is spread out alone in her own row, her hair hanging off the end into the aisle.

"You're a messy bitch," I whisper to Brad, who looks up from his book innocently.

"I don't know what you're talking about."

"I'm talking about having the balls to sleep with two friends in the same weekend."

"You knew why I came," he points out.

"Yes, but you're the one who boohooed into my boobs about being rejected by Taryn. She's the one you owe an apology to."

"For what?" he demands.

I grab my tiny empty water bottle and chuck it at him. "For thinking with your dick all weekend. You planned Charlie's bachelor party around Taryn, and then when the going got tough, you walked away and found the first willing woman to fuck instead. Then when Taryn gave you the time of day, you never came clean with her about it. What was the first thing I did when we were going to have sex?"

"Showed me your tits?" he asks seriously. I grab Chad's empty water bottle and hurl it at him.

"No, asshole, I asked if you were clean, and then I told you I had already slept with someone this weekend. If that wasn't okay with you, then you had the chance to say, 'No, Ainsley, I don't want to risk catching something since you haven't been tested since your last casual hookup.' When I told Chad, he even said, 'That's cool, Ainsley, I ate some chick out while at the pool yesterday, but I've brushed my teeth since then.'"

Brad scowls but sinks deeper into his seat. "Whatever."

"Are you fifteen or twenty-five? If I had a child with that sort of flagrant disregard for another person's feelings, I would personally flay them alive."

"Right. You, a mother. I think that might be the funniest thing you've ever said."

His words cut deeper than I want to admit, so I just give him the finger.

Elia walks past, casting a surreptitious glance around. When I catch her eye, I give her a wink, relishing how she blushes. When she gets back to her seat, I watch Charlie pull her onto his lap while blowing kisses onto her neck.

My grumpiness is no match for her giggles, and I give into a small smile.

"Besides, Ainsley, we all know you get around more than the common cold," Brad says, unable to avoid getting in one last dig.

"And?" I ask, not letting him slut shame me.

"And that's why you would be an unfit mother."

I notice Charlie has his head turned toward our conversation, and I hope he doesn't intervene.

"And? You think because I like to have sex, and I have sex with multiple men, that makes me someone who couldn't have a kid? You're off your rocker if you think that. So fuck you very much. I'm glad Taryn decided she's done with you." That manages to shut Brad up. Like the petulant child he is, Brad just folds his arms on the table in front of us and leans down to try to sleep.

It's fifteen minutes later when I'm finally relaxing into the flight. Taryn gets up and squats in the aisle beside me.

"He's wrong, you know."

"What about?" I ask.

Taryn rubs her eyes sleepily. "You will make a really awesome mom someday. Don't let this bastard convince you otherwise."

"Oh, I know. I just don't know if I'll find Mr. Right in time to make it happen."

"There are always options." Taryn squeezes my shoulder and heads to the bathroom.

I mull over what she said. I owe her a massive apology when we land, but knowing that I have someone in my corner like her, someone with such ferocious loyalty and love, convinces me that if I decide to be a mom, to do it alone, I can do this with her as part of my village.

With her words in my head, I pull out my phone and review the matches I already have on Sleepless Nights. I'm distracted by a text from my paralegal reminding me that tomorrow I have my first of likely many mediations with a couple that's dealing with infidelity and an aging cat, who is the only other being involved in this divorce. You would think that my profession would leave me jaded with love and marriage, but it only makes me want to find it for myself.

Being a mediator means I'm privy to some of the worst moments in a couple's time together, but I've also seen how important communication is. Hell, I ended a relationship over a lack of communication. It makes me want to do better. It makes me want better for myself, for my future partner and for whatever family I have, even if it's just me and a baby.

Maybe I do still have time to achieve what I want. Maybe I can find Mr. Right and have the life I had once dreamed of: career, husband and a baby.

Who cares if it's not in that order?

Acknowledgments

I think I would be remiss if I didn't right away thank my friends for throwing me a memorable bachelorette party, some pieces of which landed themselves right here in this book. Danielle, Mia, Laurie, Amy and Heather. You planned a hell of a weekend, and I wouldn't change a moment of it. Except, maybe I would have had more margaritas that first night.

There is of course a need to thank Hannah, again. When I said my previous book wouldn't exist without you, it was because you pushed me to publish. This time, it's because you told me this was a story I needed to tell, and I did. These shenanigans live on the page because of you.

I think my weirdest acknowledgement goes to Josh. You ridiculous man who never fails to be so genuine and true to yourself. It makes me smile, and I'm so glad Mike got you as his roommate Freshman year.

I can't thank my editor, Amanda, enough. You're always there, safely guiding me through potential ship wars and helping me learn and never judging.

For my mom and dad for always believing in me and always pushing me to be better.

And lastly, to Mike, always Mike, for leaning in with me, for knowing that I can do it and for never complaining even when I hid in my library to work late. Your endless support means everything to me.

For you dear reader, for taking this journey, and seeing it through.

Coming Soon

Catch the girls in the next Love in the Big Apple book...

Madison
Avenue
Mediator

After seeing her ex-fiancé get married, can divorce mediator, Ainsley Seaborn find her own happily ever after?

Available now!

Coming Soon

The Underworld needs a queen, is Daphne Hale up to the task of competing in the Calling for that title?

Book one in the Game of God's Series - The King's Game is available now!!

About the Author

Nicole Sanchez has been writing stories on any scrap of paper she could get her hands since before middle school. She lives in New Jersey with her high school sweetheart and love of her life along with their two quirky cats. When she isn't writing or wielding the Force, she can be found traveling the world with her husband or training for her next RunDisney Event.

For more books and updates:

Newsletter

Website

Facebook Reader Group

Also by Nicole Sanchez

Love in the Big Apple Series:
Central Park Collision
Las Vegas Luck
Madison Avenue Mediator

Game of Gods Series:
The King's Game
The Queen's Gamble
The Royal Gauntlet

Anthologies:
Billionaires and Babes Charity Anthology
Getting Witchy With It Charity Anthology
No Going Back: Sultry in the City Anthology

Made in the USA
Monee, IL
07 August 2023

40630245R00075